Contents

parmesan, pond and police 3

ribcage and eggs 13

abuse and desire 23

reg, reason and the raisin 32

the french revelation 48

threats and settlements.................................55

pierre and passports 68

punch and tea 75

the end of the cheese.................................79

shock and suspicion................................85

the case of halibut 96

murder meetings 104

the bleach-parsleys................................113

press and impressionists 128

pub and passion 137

exposed members 148

clamp and cuffs 157

tears, shed 171

kids and a nose 180

passion and desire 193

GW00402067

The Cheese Murder
By Nick Willson

www.cheesemurder.co.uk

First Published in Great Britain in 2009 by Lees Media Limited
Copyright © Nick Willson 1991 – 2009

ISBN 978-1-906866-34-1

Published by Lees Media Limited
www.leesmedia.co.uk

chapter one
parmesan, pond and police

Ralph Parmesan always fought for what he wanted. He was objectionable, obstinate and obstreperous. But for his faults, he had succeeded in winning over the affections of the steamiest girl in Larynx. This was a prime example of his dogged determinations, his pure self-willed drive.

Ralph was medium height, solid but lanky with a hard, menacing face, topped with a lumpy mat of mousey hair.

For someone with such a tenacity for self-fulfilment, he may be viewed with some derision for being just a bus driver. But his purpose was rational. He was due to marry Christine Ribcage, a girl of many assets, not least her bloated bank balance. Her generous agreement to share part of her funds with Ralph, allowing him unlimited access to one of her bank accounts, gave him the freedom to perform almost any occupation of his desire.

He always loved buses: he can recall his rides on the trolley-bus circuits as a young boy; those upreaching traction poles connecting machine to power, dictating direction with a romantic, sleek, silken grace. He often remembered the time, when he was just seven, when he jumped off the platform of a trolley-bus whilst it was gliding its course through the bustling high street in Sockwith. He had forgotten to buy his mother a birthday card on behalf of his father (a mission for reasons explained later) and, on impulse, had dived from the exit, reeling through the air, finally landing sprawled over a pram. Its contents, one baby and a bag of Macfisheries groceries, pelleted through Timothy Whites doorway, their descent cushioned by a prostrate, elderly gentleman trying a pack of insoles in his old shoes for size.

Needless to say, Ralph hadn't stayed around to witness the

mayhem. His mother had read him the story a few days later in *The Sockwith Weekly,* describing the injurious repercussions of the *"young thug's actions"* in horrifyingly graphic and exaggerated detail.

Ralph, as on that occasion, has never admitted to any of his less than honourable deeds - which amount to tens, if not hundreds, of dastardly pranks. But for all that, the 25-year-old excelled at his job. The management at Sockwith Corporation Transport had delighted in Ralph's enthusiasm. They'd often watch him mount the driver's seat at early dawn, his expression advertising a deep love for the Metropolitan Integral Double Decker, as if he was chauffering a leather-clad limousine.

One afternoon in early December 1991, the management at Sockwith Corporation Transport was conducting a crisis meeting. A meeting that would shape Ralph's destiny. Advances in technology, imperative improvements and general rising costs had led to a discussion of the deepest ferocity.

"We need to cut staff!" the Chief Accountant repeatedly insisted. "We have no choice. No choice at all"

"So you keep saying," the Operations Manager huffed in his brash Yorkshire accent. "Yes, the older buses have to go and yes we need to get up-to-date with those new-fangled ones," he continued, bashing the boardroom table with his fists, his temper close to boiling. "But if we cut the drivers, we won't have enough of them for the new bloody buses, will we?"

"You miss the point, Archie," stressed the Accountant, nervously fidgeting his bow tie. "To pay for the new buses, we'll need to slim down the timetables on the less cost-effective routes and maximise on the profitable ones. Can't you see, we *need* to cut staff!"

"If you say *'we need to cut staff'* one more bloody time, I'll swing for you! You think you have all the flash answers, with your posh bloody college background, your ridiculous bow-tie, your stupid braces! But you can't get it into your head that if you cut the timetables, you won't need the bloody buses, will you?!"

Archie Pond's irritation was bringing his crimson, balding skull close to detonation. The Operations Manager could feel spasms of raging heat enveloping his every feature. His ears felt like two deep-fried crispy pancakes preparing to ooze their piping-hot secretions. His eyes were red and sore and protruded so viciously, his eyelids were close to cracking.

His dramatic, emotive reactions to the Accountant's destructive witterings were deep-rooted. He'd lived his entire adult life for the buses. He was one of the few that shared Ralph Parmesan's passion and dreaded the prospect of change. And he knew that, if the changes went ahead, both he and Ralph were likely to be hived off with a meagre brown envelope carrying nothing more than a paltry pay-off: a sum that would be a grave offence to their devotion and commitment.

He knew that, for Ralph, even though only in his mid-twenties (Archie was 55), such an action would be a devastating assault on his very being. It were these beliefs and fears that had generated such a blood-boiling intensity.

A third man in the room interjected. This was the Chief Executive, Arbuthnot Clamp, hired just a few months back, headhunted by SCT and plucked from Griswald's, a local pie factory. He was recognised for his dictatorial manner, his narrow-mindedness and ultimate desire to make money regardless of human strife.

"Shut up, Archie!" snapped the Chief. "If you don't calm down this minute, I'll fire you, understand?"

There was silence.

Then Archie inhaled the deepest breath imaginable, wheezed, spluttered and slumped back in his chair. His eyes rotated a bit, his eyelids retracted, displaying momentary stretch marks and his rough, purple lips trembled. He wanted to speak. He wanted to tell the savage Fidel Castro lookalike, Arbuthnot Clamp, where he could ram his new-fangled buses. But his throat was constricting amidst a tempestuous convulsion. His eyeballs continued to circulate tightly in their sockets. He could vaguely hear the Accountant and Chief Executive through a piercing whistle that had incised its way beyond both ear drums.

His eyes turned damp. His sinuses imploded and in one ginormous moment, the Yorkshireman expelled a terrifying groan, leapt to his feet, jolted and then collapsed thunderously onto the boardroom table, falling face-first onto the water jug. Huge splinters of glass lodged into his temple, penetrating his cheekbones and a dormant teaspoon catapulted with shocking velocity into his right ear hole, totally consuming the handle. In that one horrifying instant every piece of paper, pen, cup, saucer and jug had bounced off the solid oak table as if an earthquake had struck. The impact was deafening. It was carnage.

"Well. Well, well, well," muttered Clamp. "What is the world coming to, eh? What's wrong with this man, eh, Accountant? Get him off my table. Now we'll need to find cash for a new jug and spoon, won't we?"

The Accountant seemed to be fixed to the wall. He was trembling. His jaw quivered, his chin rubbing his large, flamboyant bow-tie, causing its shape to simulate a large butterfly trying to fly.

"Accountant!!" screamed Clamp.

"Uh?"

"Accountant! .. get that fat lump off my table ... Now!!"

The Accountant sprung into life, sprinting three times round the room like a police helicopter circling a major incident.

"What in God's name are you doing?" shrieked Clamp.

"I'm... I'm trying to work out the best way to get Archie up. What do I do?"

"Grab him under his stinking armpits and drag him off! Just get him out of here!" Then Clamp emulated the Accountant, encircling the site of devastation. His brash expression suddenly dissolved, his thin greying beard appearing to whiten with a sudden, stricken concern. He stopped.

"Oh Christ, " he whispered. "He's dead."

The Cheese Murder   6

"I thought you knew that, sir," choked the Accountant. He then realised that the Chief was in shock. "Sit down, sir. I'll get you some water and ring for an ambulance".

"Right." Arbuthnot Clamp slowly dragged back his chair, placing it into the corner furthest from the site of carnage. He sat motionless for minutes, bolt upright, hands on knees, staring at Archie's crumpled body. The teaspoon was awash with blood, hardly visible against a backdrop of deep red liquid which had trickled out of Archie's ear, over his lacerated cheek, down his chin and was now dripping onto his tired Hush Puppies, surrounded by a pool of water.

Clamp arose, slowly, and approached the body. He pushed his face towards Archie's, inquisitively. He had noticed something nestling under his shattered nose amongst the fragments of glass. It was Archie's calculator. Archie always took his calculator to meetings. It was an instrument, Archie always thought, that implied intelligence and numeracy: something to enhance his rather drab, rotund exterior. Something, however, he didn't have a clue how to operate.

His nose was curled across the once grey buttons and all that was visible amongst the flesh, blood, water and glass, was the bottom row of digits. The 'equals' button had somehow been dislodged in the violent landing.

"Christ," muttered Clamp. "What a mess".

He sprawled himself over Archie's back, inserted his hands under Archie's arms and pulled. Archie was a man of generous proportions. "Come on, come on," breathed Clamp. He steadied himself once more, holding his breath and heaved at the body. The weight and the mess was too much. "Sod it. Where's the damn'd ambulance?"

He glanced down at his damp hands. They exhibited a thin film of blood and sweat. With a sort of dispassionate revulsion, he wiped them with one sweep of his palms over the dead man's hunched shoulders.

Just then the Accountant came running in, breathless. "I've... I've rung 999... they'll be here any minute now. They told me to make sure he isn't moved."

"Great," replied Clamp. "I almost had a hernia trying to get him off my table."

"You've moved him then?" questioned the Accountant.

"Hardly. He's too messy, fat and horrid... I just tried pulling him off.. I think his head's moved a bit: you can see more of the calculator now."

"Calculator?"

"Yes. I noticed it under his nose. Look - in that pool there," Clamp continued, pointing. "It's got a button missing. I don't know where it is."

"Could be anywhere amongst all this mess..."

"Never mind. We'll find it later," tutted Clamp as if it was of the utmost importance. "It was a Corporation one you know".

"What?"

"The calculator."

"Oh."

"Its *our* property," Clamp mercilessly insisted. "It belongs to us. We have to account for everything. You should know that, you're the Accountant."

"Yes, but its only a calcula..."

"Only?!" interrupted the Chief. "Its an asset. When we find that damn' button I'll get one of our mechanics to clean it up and repair it. We can't waste property you know!"

"Unless it's uneconomical to repair of course..." argued the Accountant.

"Oh shut up!" snapped the Chief, gruffly. "Where's that ambulance? I've got another meeting here in ten minutes - with the Council Treasury Department - they're not going to want to sit around this heap, are they?"

Two men scuttled into the room wearing luminous yellow jackets and brandishing medical bags.

"Right, where is he?" said one.

"*Where is he?*" repeated the Chief in disbelief. "Do you mean the corpse? Oh, he just went down the shops for some teabags. He'll be back in a minute if you want to wait!"

Clamp watched the two ambulance men as they approached the body. "Oh, you've found him, then," continued Clamp with disdain.

"I'm sorry," said one of the men, "I'm afraid he's dead".

"*Dead???*" screamed Clamp. "No! You've got that wrong! He's just having a little kip. He'll be up and about in a minute talking his normal drivel, you'll see. Look! Did I see him flinch? Oh, yes, he'll be up and about in a minute!"

The two men in yellow glared at Clamp. "What are you staring at, you idiots! *Of course he's dead! Now get him out of my room! Now!*"

"Sir, sit down," the Accountant muttered, comfortingly, putting his arm round Clamp's shoulders.

"Get your stinking arm off me and get out!"

"But I'm needed for the next meeting," trembled the Accountant, flicking the wings of his bow-tie anxiously.

"*Just bugger off!*" yelled Clamp, pointing aggressively to the door. The Accountant went.

Two police arrived.

"I'm Detective Inspector Brian Fluids and this is Constable Vivian Fledgling," introduced a smartly dressed middle-aged man, flapping his badge and squeezing between Clamp and the ambulance men.

"He's dead, sir," stated one of the ambulance men.

"Bloody hell," mumbled Clamp, resigning himself to his corner chair.

"Right. And you are...?" approached Fluids.

"I am what?" retorted Clamp.

"Your name, sir. What's your name?"

"I'm the Chief Executive of this bus operation. My name is Arbuthnot Clamp," spat the Chief.

"Clamp? How do you spell that?"

"C L A M P. Clamp. Okay?"

"Oh, as in Wheelclamp?" mused the officer.

"Very funny. Very funny. Now can you get that heap of death out of my room and get the place cleaned up. I've got visitors in two minutes."

"I'm sorry, sir. I can't do that yet. We need to study things very closely before we move anything."

"What the hell do you need to study closely? He's dead! If you study him closely, do you think he'll suddenly bounce into life and do a Morris Dance?!"

"Would you like a cup of tea, Mr Clamp?" came a soft, feminine voice. Constable Fledgling leant in front of him smiling sweetly. "I'll get you a cuppa and we'll go to another room if you like and have a quiet chat. What do you say?"

Her calm tone seemed to work.

"Er, no I won't have a tea. It tastes like dog piss. I'll have some of the soup," he said, pointing towards the corridor.

"Soup? Out of the machine?" Fledgling inquired. "What flavour?"

"There's only one flavour. I don't know what it's meant to be - it doesn't say but it tastes marginally better than everything else."

"Right."

"Here," Clamp fumbled in his trouser pocket and rattled through a mountain of loose change. Here's 10p. That's enough for mine."

"Oh. Right. Thanks." Fledgling left the room.

"Go with her, sir," DI Fluids suggested to Clamp. "It'll be less stressful away from this room. I'll catch up with you later. Oh, by the way: the other chap that witnessed the incident. Do you know where he is?"

"No," replied Clamp and left the room, turning to glare once more at the industrious medical men pouring over the body as if they were looking for the on-off switch.

"Is he still dead?" yelled Clamp from halfway down the corridor.

Clamp stood for a few seconds, looking down through the

canteen window at the congregating staff in the station yard. Around thirty men and women were motioning up at the board room, pointing, gesticulating as if they were dramatising the incident themselves.

"This sort of news travels fast doesn't it?" came the female Constable's voice behind him. "Here's your soup. Is it meant to be that colour?"

Clamp took the thin corrugated plastic cup from her and raised it to his lips, blowing gently into the peppery pink steam. He was still concentrating on the animated crowd below.

"I wonder what they're saying. I bet that bloody Accountant's been shooting his mouth off and now they'll all think it was my fault that wretched man died. Just look at them, pointing, chattering. Look, there's even more of them joining in now! Lazy! They're all lazy!" he puffed. "Anything to skive off work. I'll have to go down there and sort them out."

"You may want to think about closing down the depot for the rest of the day, Mr Clamp. As a sign of respect as much as anything..."

"No way! That's not how to run a successful business. How will our passengers get about if we close down? Customer satisfaction. Customer satisfaction."

"All right, sir. I'll tell you what, can we find a quiet room to talk in and I'll get someone to sort out your people. Do you have a statement or a message that someone could relay to them so that they understand what has happened?"

"Er, yes. Write this down and get one of your officers to read it out to them over the PA system."

"Okay." Fledgling produced her notebook. "Right, what's the message?"

"Er..." Clamp slurped his soup and swirled the remnants about in the base of the cup. He thought carefully, continuing to agitate the cup. "Er... Right. Take this down. Er .. *Archie's dead. Now get back to bloody work!*"

"Is that it, Mr Clamp?"

"Yep. That sums it up, doesn't it? The PA system's in my

office just down there."

DC Fledgling disappeared with the message. Clamp continued to watch the amassing throng from the window. His attention was distracted by the sight of a man who had leapt out of his bus and was now running madly across the station forecourt towards the crowd. After a few seconds' conversation, he moved on, pushing through the Press and police and vanishing out of view into the stairway under the canteen.

"Who's that?" Clamp muttered to himself. He could hear the man's footsteps charging up the stairs towards him. The figure appeared at the canteen door.

It was Ralph Parmesan.

chapter two
ribcage and eggs

Christine Ribcage was a beautiful 24-year old. Financial issues posed no problem but the most domestic and routine chores wrought sad neglect. Her past romantic entanglements included a Frenchman, Pierre LePants, who was frequently violent, followed by an over-possessive, infatuated charmer, Leonard Mantlepiece. Now she lived with Ralph Parmesan but her relationship was becoming increasingly rocky.

At four o'clock she arrived home from her few hours' work at the Larynx Village Olde Tea Shoppe. Christine helped out more to occupy her time than for financial reward. She had won a national competition two years back and invested the £250,000 prize money, living mainly off the interest. The competition had comprised of visiting a local show home on a new estate near Sockwith, inspecting the bathroom carefully and then to place in order of importance the many features the bathroom offered. Of course, the all-important tie-breaker was the key. She remembers clearly, to this day, her completion of the slogan: *I'd like a Scratchings Stain-Free Bathroom because...*
She had ingeniously added the words: "*it would be nice to have.*"
Her stunning, concise and direct response earned her £200,000 plus a bonus £50,000 for posing naked for a tasteful Scratchings Stain-Free Bathroom ad campaign.
She had little shame. Her direct approach to life, incurring all facets of self-centred enjoyment had, for the most part, made her an ideal match for her fiancée, Ralph Parmesan, Both partners were individualists. They each highly valued their freedom and independence, which, in their case was the bonding agent.
Aware of the attraction generated by her riches, Christine had laid down a set of simple conditions as a sort of security

measure. She still had virtually every penny that she had won. She had no idea how her excessive funds could be expended - materialism meant little to her. Whilst she had conceded to share one bank account with Ralph, she insisted that he must always work and support himself in the pleasures he enjoyed - mainly drinking - and that he must pay the mortgage on his property. His access to the account must be limited to justifiable, personally unaffordable expenses. She checked her bank statements with thorough precision and required detailed accounts of any transactions initiated by Ralph.

Parmesan really prided himself on his relationship with Christine (although he didn't always show it) , the envy of many a single man in Larynx, and was therefore satisfied with her financial conditions. Many of his cynical rivals perceived his intentions as downright dishonourable, surmising that once married to her, within the month, he would surrender his affections and devise a scheme to procure her money.

They lived in a small limestone semi-detached cottage in Church Lane. Whitewashed exterior walls, dusty leaded windows, partly shrouded by ivy and firethorn, ancient wizened rose bushes muddled with overgrown shrubs, guiding the stone pathway from a warped wooden gate to a warped front door.

The house complemented the village perfectly. Larynx was a typical, sleepy village that displayed immense charm, reflecting the sort of 19th century Englishness that would have suited Miss Marple and delight American tourists. It had three pubs, a general store, the tea shop and the crotchety old church of Saint Barnaby, few structures still adhering to the rules of perpendicular.

Having stoked the fading lounge fire into life, Christine shuffled about in the kitchen investigating the assortment of cupboards for culinary inspiration. Her expertise in this field was limited to the most elementary meals but she always endeavoured to present Ralph with a reasonably creative concoction, if not particularly edible.

"Eggs, yes eggs", she muttered, the fridge light illuminating her pretty features and sending a shimmer across her long, shaggy blonde hair. She continued fumbling in the fridge. "Ah, cheese... a tomato... courgettes... lettuce..." She extracted each piece, clutching them in her hands, thinking of a suitable dish to create.

"Omelette. Yes, an omelette."

She proceeded to manoeuvre Ralph's treasured cans of lager around the fridge shelves, in search of further ingredients, picking up a scrunched delicatessen bag. Inquisitively, she un-taped it and reached inside. "Oh yes! It's that kipper!"

Her glossy lips shone in the light as she smiled at the prospect of delivering an omelette of some uniqueness to her Ralph, dreaming of a rare cosy evening by the open fire: a delicious golden brown, sizzling omelette accompanied by a glass of foaming, chilled pilsner lager and cuddles.

Six o'clock arrived and Ralph came clattering through the front doorway, stumbling and cursing.

"Is that you, Ralph?" called Ribcage from the kitchen, her creation almost complete.

"What's that foul stench?!" yelled Parmesan swaying into the kitchen.

"Do you mean dinner, Ralphy? It's a special surprise omelette, finely honed by my..." She paused, looking over at him.

"What's up, darling? You look dreadful. What's happened?"

She walked towards him. He turned his back and proceeded to pace up and down the living room, overtly upset, swinging his bus driver's hat like a pendulum.

"I've been down the pub."

"That's nothing new. What's happened? Ralph, what is it? Tell me," she insisted, trying to block his frantic route around the room.

Then he stopped. He studied the badge on his hat as if requiring it to generate the words he needed.

"Archie," he spluttered. He coughed, expelling a vocal blockage. "It's Archie. He's dead".

"What?"

Ralph amplified the statement: "Dead! That bloody Clamp did it. I swear he did it. I don't know how but..."

"What happened?"

Ralph's brow folded, either to curtail tears or to summon a calculated account of the incident. He sniffed noisily. "He was in a meeting with Clamp and that snotty Accountant. I know it was about job losses and I know Archie would do anything to save our jobs."

He slammed his hat onto the marble fire surround, in a motion assimilating the crack of a judge's gavel passing finite judgement: "They must have had a row. Those two shits slaughtered him!"

"They wouldn't get away with it, surely?" challenged Christine. "Let me get you a beer. Sit down."

Ralph Parmesan sat. The beer can spat open and he swigged and gulped furiously. "There was a right carry-on at the depot: press, plod, ambulances, all sorts. Clamp wouldn't even shut down the station for the rest of the day!" He waved the can around as he spoke, maintaining its vertical requirements with perfection.

He swigged and sniffed again. "I managed to get in to see Castro while the plod were out the room. I went up to him. I said *'you killed him, didn't you! You killed him and just because he wanted to protect us – our jobs!'*. I prodded him. I wanted him to admit it. I wanted him to break down and grovel at my feet. He just stared at me, cold and still and then he just said *'No, he just died'*. I mean, why should he *just die?* Don't you think it's a coincidence that he *just died* in the middle of some heated meeting about issues he cared so much for? He was the one man we could trust, rely on. Now he's bloody dead!"

Ralph finished the drink, crushed the can with one hand whilst squeezing his ruffled fair hair with the other, trying to make sense of it all.

"Oh, Ralph. What's going to happen now? Is your job safe?"

His thoughts were diverted: "What *is* that awful smell?"

"Oh, no!" she exclaimed, swivelling and running into the kitchen. "Oh, no! My lovely golden omelettes! Ruined! I was really looking forward to them."

She whipped them from under the grill where they had been browning and bubbling, now smoking and crisped.

"Omelettes?" queried Ralph, staring over her shoulder at the blackened mess, resembling the smouldering debris from an autumnal bonfire.

"I'm sorry, Ralph. I'd carefully hand-picked some really exciting ingredients for these: cheese, tomatoes, kippers, onions, lettuce..."

"Kippers and lettuce in an omelette?" snorted Ralph, appearing more mystified by this than the day's tragedy. "The best place for them's the bin, burnt or not, if you ask me! You really do come up with some crap meals, do you know that, woman?!"

The meal shattered into the bin and he reached for another can.

"Forget dinner. I'm going down the pub. I've had a shit day. My best mate at work's snuffed it and so has my wretched dinner. I'm going."

Ralph headed for the front door, again swigging. The door rattled open and slammed shut.

"Bugger, I didn't make any pudding," she muttered to herself.

She heaped the used jugs, knives, frying pans and grill pan into the sink, the culinary instruments randomly piled into a mini-mountain like a car scrap heap. She flopped onto the sofa in resignation.

The telephone rang. "Hello?".

"Hello, it's Sockwith Police here. Are you Mrs Parmesan?" came the tinny voice down the line.

"No, I'm not, we're not married. I expect you want to speak

to Ralph, do you?"

"Yes please... er, who are you then?"

"I'm Christine Ribcage, Ralph's girlfriend."

"Oh. Well, can I speak to Mr Parmesan, please?"

"Well no, not really."

"Oh? And why not?"

"Well, he's not here. He's gone out."

"It's rather important we speak to him tonight, Miss Ribcage. Do you know where he's gone?"

"For a drink. I don't know which pub."

"Well, we'd rather you brought him home so we could have a chat with him there. Otherwise we'll have to go out and find him."

"All right. I'll telephone the pubs and see if I can get him home."

"Right. We're on our way. Don't worry, he's not being arrested," the voice said with vague reassurance.

Christine rang the three pubs. She knew the numbers off-by-heart. It was a regular occurrence, tracking him down, normally to plead with him to return home for dinner. Her requests seldom succeeded. His preference for lager outshone any meal that Ribcage could ever create, regardless of available ingredients, cooking instructions or divine inspiration.

"Good evening. The Foot and Mouth Arms..."

"Is Ralph there, please?"

"No, not tonight, Chris," came the immediate response.

"The Blunt Raisin? Is Ralph there, please?"

"No, sorry, Chris".

She tried the last option, the Grinning Plank.

"Yes, Christine, he's at the bar right here. Hold on..."

"Ralph?"

"Yeah." He rolled his eyes and slurred his words: "Don't tell me you've made another meal? What is it this time: horse shit flan, or is it another kipper surprise?"

"Listen!" snapped Christine. "It's the police. They're

coming round here in a minute to see you. I told them I'd try and get hold of you, otherwise they were going to fetch you from the pub. It must be something to do with Archie."

Ralph frustratingly agreed to surrender his pint and trudged home. He arrived as the police arrived. They ushered him into his home. The more senior officer was Brian Fluids, in smart plain clothes, his colleague, Constable Stringent in full uniform, the latter a strange-looking chap with comic features unbecoming of his profession.

Fluids introduced them. "Thanks for coming home. I realise you must have had a bad day with Mr Pond dying and all that."

"Do you want a cup of coffee?" offered Ribcage to the two officers. "Yes, please" they said in unison and she disappeared into the kitchen.

She clattered amongst the grease-laden washing up and extricated two mugs, each displaying black viscous rings and coffee stains, residues from breakfast time.

Stringent added, "We just want to ask a few questions, Mr Parmesan," raising his voice above the kitchen's din. "You knew Archie well?"

"Yeah," replied Ralph, removing his coat, picking up the poker and prodding the radiant coal in the fireplace. He turned to face the men, brandishing the iron stick aggressively, like a sword about to pierce any doubters in the room. "I knew him well. We were the best of mates at work. We were called the 'Bus Brothers'. People took the piss because we had such passion for buses. Most of the others just did it because it was a job. But Archie... well... "

He paused, replacing the poker in its holder, picking up his warm hat from the mantle and stroking it proudly. "Archie was one of the old school. He really cared about the way the station was run; not just for himself but for all us workers."

"And particularly you?"

"Yes, I suppose so. Because we were the only ones that really loved it."

"I've never been on a bus thingy," stated the odd-looking Stringent curiously, "What's it like?"

Fluids hastily repaired the conversation, noticing Ralph's slightly drunken eyes targeting the poker once more. "Err, Ralph. We believe you spoke to Clamp shortly after the incident. Is that right?"

"Yep," he replied defiantly. "I heard what had happened - the news came through on my radio as I was completing the number 47 round. Archie told me this morning how he was dreading the meeting – that is would end up 'as an accountant's dream and a worker's nightmare'. That's exactly what he'd said. Archie had said it a lot recently. He could feel it in his bones. Things were beginning to go down hill at work with the new boss."

"Do you want milk?" came a cry from the industrious caterer in the kitchen.

"Please," called the officers.

"Oh," came a disheartened mutter. Christine prized open the wings of an old, yellowing milk carton using one of the knives discarded after cooking and still bearing evidence of the various vegetables for which it had been employed. The milk carton, started well over a week ago, had remained concealed behind a stack of blown yoghurts and only discovered during the omelette-making ceremony. The fresh milk had been used earlier. She raised the tatty spout to her nose, flinched and shook it vigorously. A piece of onion which had departed the knife, flipped and plopped into the curdled liquid. She didn't even bother asking about their sugar requirements - there was certainly none on-site.

"Go on, Ralph," prompted Fluids.

"Well, that's it, really. I knew there was going to be trouble and the next I hear he's dead. He just *happened to drop dead* in front of the two men who were out to wreck our jobs!" Ralph rotated again to face the fire and began wafting the flames into action with his hat. The radiance oscillated floods of orange onto his face, punctuating the hard panels of his cheeks and squarish chin.

He sighed. "I decided to go straight back to the bus station and catch Clamp in his office. I spotted him up in the canteen. He was just standing there. Really calm."

"What did you say to him then?"

"I just told him that I knew he must have killed Archie. I wanted him to admit it. I wanted to bloody smack him one!"

A teaspoon frantically rattled round the mugs in the kitchen as Christine fished out the slithers of onion and tried to disperse the clotted lumps of mustard-coloured milk.

"Well, sir, it's *our* job to establish exactly how Mr Pond died," stressed Fluids. "We expect to know by the morning but the signs seem to suggest a heart attack. We would ask that you do not approach Mr Clamp until this matter is resolved. If you do, it is likely to get you into trouble."

Christine Ribcage appeared, a mug in each hand. "Here's your coffee."

She offered the first to the young Stringent, cleverly attempting to cast her shadow over the cup to obscure its stale contents. He tried to clutch it by the handle, already gripped by Christine's hand. His hand proceeded to mimic a maypole dance around the mug in an attempt to avoid grasping it fully, aware of its immense heat.

"Got it, I think..." he said unconvincingly. In a split second, the mug hurtled to the rug below, the oily beverage splattering and fuming over his shining shoes and trouser legs. "Sorry," he grinned inanely. "I thought I'd got it."

The hostess hurriedly thrust the other mug at Fluids and she dashed to the kitchen for a towel.

Fluids took a sip, hesitated and swallowed reluctantly. He wiped his teeth with his thumb, erasing several lumps resembling rice pudding. He gingerly placed the mug on the mantle top. "Lovely... thanks," he called politely, his tongue angling for further chunks.

"Is there anything else you can tell us that you think is important?" Fluids continued, his fingers darting in and out of his mouth, retrieving further spots of sour, stagnant scum.

"Not really," replied Ralph "But I'll say this: Clamp's trouble. You do your job properly and you'll see I'm right."

Christine by this stage was on all fours frantically rubbing the rug, Stringent's shoes and his trouser legs with a cardigan that had been queuing for the washing machine for several days. Stringent just stood there beaming boyishly, as if the experience of a young lady scouring his ankles was some unfulfilled erotic fantasy.

"Right, we'll be off then," summed up Fluids. "Come on, Stan... Stan... Stan!"

"Uh?" Stan Stringent awoke from his delirious diversion. "Oh, yes, right, err, thanks, umm .. thanks then..."

Christine arose and Stringent bent down, rearranging his ruffled trouser legs, recognising that his moment of pleasure was at an end. "Thanks then, Miss Ribcage for your... umm, your..."

"Come on, Stringent!" snapped Fluids and they turned towards the front door. "If there's anything else, Ralph, do get in touch," advised DI Fluids as he reached for the latch.

chapter three
abuse and desire

With Christmas fast approaching Larynx was bustling with locals flitting back and forth for their festive wares. The general store was enjoying record trade in Christmas puddings and decorations. An old green truck had assumed its annual position by the church gates, overflowing with freshly-sawn Christmas trees. The sky was heavy, low and grey, preparing for an explosion of snow, like a volcano giving warning of imminent eruption. The older parishioners were engaged in the customary duties of hanging up bunting and lights, purchased for the Silver Jubilee and shamelessly advertising their age, ladders upstanding on trees and edifices.

The younger folk took little notice of these seasonal enhancements. Their interests focussed more on doubling their visits to the public houses and trebling their intake of alcohol.

The Grinning Plank was the most popular for the younger generation - those who had come of age up to around 30. Anyone more senior was driven out by silence and stares.

Parmesan had taken up his usual position at the bar. He had his own crystal tankard, stored behind the bar when unemployed, with his name scratched round it. The bar stool may well have been similarly labelled for him. Ralph rarely spoke to any of the other regulars - a nod of the head when he entered and little else during the rest of his occupancy. His pleasure seemed to be singularly placed on the brew that so delighted him, sucked out of the most outrageously ostentatious pump on the bar, resembling a futuristic fruit machine, with flickering neon shapes and emblazoned with the words: *CRUSTS ORIGINAL PILSNER*. The liquid it spat out with such boisterous effervesence wholly complemented the tasteless promotional electric pump.

In the corner directly behind Parmesan was a trio of raucous lads in their twenties. One of them, the most reserved by their standards, rose from his chair and announced: "Right, I'm getting another pint. Anyone else want one?"

An immediate cheer went up, sounding more like a football crowd than just his two companions. "Another pint of Old Blagger for me, please mate," came one voice. "Same for me, Lenny! Cheers!" came the other.

Lenny approached the bar and inserted himself between Ralph and another chap. "All right, Ralph?" greeted Lenny reticently. Parmesan ignored him, sinking his face back into his tankard.

"Yes, Len?" prompted the barman.

"Err, two pints of Baggins' Old Blagger and I'll have, err..." He studied the badges on the five handpumps, erect and dignified. "I'll try the Slappers, please, Bert."

"Stoat or Weasel?"

"Err ... what's the O.G.?"

Parmesan snorted and shook his head. He'd so often witnessed these lads taking minutes to finalise their guest brew purchases, based on original gravity and regional origin. He could not comprehend the enthusiasm stimulated by a range of real ales: some that looked like warm foaming pond water and others that looked suspiciously like Marmite, save for their crowning lather. Ralph tightly hugged his tankard of aerated juice, symbolising their uncomplicated relationship.

"Stoat is 1042 and Weasel 1050," replied Bert, the barman. "Oh, Weasel, then," concluded Lenny instantly.

Bert tugged three times at the strong handle and the dark brew smoothly filled the glass to the brim, curls of froth spilling over into the ullage tray. Lenny took a sip, his length of eyebrow elevating with pleasure. "Oh, yes", he commented in adoration, his tongue sliding smoothly round his lips. "Gorgeous! Is this from the West Country, by any chance, Bert?"

"Yeah; it's a new independent Somerset Brewery. Glad you like it, Len."

Once more, Parmesan showed complete irreverence, contemptuously muttering into his Crusts. Leonard Mantlepiece expertly carried the three rich brews to his table of chums and sat down.

"That Parmesan gets right up my nose. Ignorant pillock," punctuated Leonard.

"I know what you mean," replied Reg between voluminous gulps of Old Blagger.

"God knows how he managed to get Christine," continued Leonard sorrowfully, reflecting on his loss.

"Don't start getting melancholy," interjected the third lad, Bob Rack, foreseeing a morbid soliloquy unless the theme of conversation quickly changed track. But Leonard had started: "He's a turd. What the hell has he got that I didn't have?" he continued, reflecting further. "I was kind, thoughtful, generous, loving... all that stuff. And look at him. He's ugly, rude, has no interests except boring buses and crap lager... all he wants is her riches."

"Keep your voice down, Len," warned Reg, his eyes cautiously flickering up towards the boney figure of Parmesan perched on his stool. "Anyway, you don't know he's just after her money. You just think that because he's such a plonker."

"You know, sometimes I really wish I was a thug; that I had the guts to flatten him," snarled Lenny.

"Yes, and thankfully you're not like that. Otherwise we wouldn't be your best mates, would we?" reasoned Bob, wrapping his arm round Lenny's shoulders and squeezing him warmly.

"Yeah," sighed Leonard. He studied the remains of his pint and smiled. "You know what?"

"What?" the friends replied.

"This beer is absolutely gorgeous!" He studied it further, took another gulp, burped, smiled and wiped his lips with his wrist. He raised the glass high above his head, cleared his throat and vociferously introduced it. "SLAPPERS WEASEL!" he announced with pride. The threesome applauded loudly.

Bert picked up the telephone on the bar. "Hello, Grinning Plank... yes, yes he is, Christine... hold on..." and passed the phone to Ralph.

Leonard's ears pricked up. He watched and listened. "Shh, lads for a minute: she's on the phone to him again." He strained his ears.

"What do you want now?" Ralph spat pugnaciously. "You've got *what* made for dinner? Celery and Old Oak Ham Curry?! You've gotta be joking! No! No bloody way, Chris... I'd rather starve ..." His voice faded behind a clamour at the far end of the bar. Leonard creased up his smooth face, listening with all his might. He was still fanatical about Christine, even after almost a year without her.

The pub quietened: "No!" Parmesan shouted, "Can't you get it into your stupid head? I don't want that crap! In fact, you might as well hang up your bloody oven gloves for good... I don't care if you bought the celery fresh from the market.. I don't give a rat's arse any more... NO!.. Just sod off and leave me in peace!!" He contemptuously thrust the phone back at Bert.

Bob and Reg were watching Leonard uncomfortably. Lenny was visibly and predictably incensed by the crude abuse fired at his beloved ex-girlfriend. His mild temperament had suddenly been aggravated into a rare, raw rage. Ralph's behaviour was a personal affront.

"I've had enough of this," Lenny huffed, his slightly drunken eyes fixed firmly on the offender. He lit a cigarette and writhed, willing himself to summon the nerve to attack Parmesan head-on.

"Don't, Lenny," his mates repeatedly pleaded. Leonard stood up, inhaled heavily and started to walk. Parmesan turned his head towards the approaching man. Reg and Bob quickly leapt to their feet, grabbed Lenny and hastily pulled him towards the exit.

"Come on, Len, calm down! It's not worth it, old mate," comforted Reg as they stepped out into the cold air.

The snow was daintily falling, only visible in the halos created by the old white street lights and the newly installed multi-coloured Christmas lanterns adorning the village square.

Reg and Bob escorted Leonard away from the pub. Lenny then pulled himself away from their grip.

"I'll see you tomorrow," he called and ran off.

He ran past the Foot and Mouth Arms, merriment emitting from the walls, past the silent church of St Barnaby and round the corner into Church Lane, lined by a row of thatched cottages and terraced houses. He slowed and stopped at one, pausing to reason with his impulsive desire to knock on the door. He looked up momentarily at the black sky, the snowflakes lightly wetting his face. Then, looking back down, he saw a faint silhouette at the leaded window, accompanied by a frail weeping. Without further consideration, he pushed at the gate, stomped up to the door and knocked.

"Go away!" came an emotional cry from inside.

"It's Lenny, Chris." he called, his ear to the craggy wood.

"Lenny?"

"Yes... Look, can I come in for a minute? I know you're upset but.." Leonard was hurriedly trying to think of a justifiable reason for his imposition.

A bolt slid back and the door opened a few inches.

Christine's face was awash with tears and smudged eyeliner. "Lenny? What are you doing here?"

"Let me in Chris, please," he urged, feeling physically weakened at the sight of her misery. She turned submissively and walked into the lounge. He followed, closing the door and keeping his distance. They stopped at opposite ends of the room, both looking at the floor in silence. The lights were dim and the fire was out. A pungent smell hung in the dank, frigid air.

"Celery and Old Oak Ham curry?" asked Lenny intuitively, gently smirking.

"How do you know?" she sniffed.

"I'm sorry, Chris but I was in the Plank and heard everything." He brushed back his dark floppy hair with his hand as if ashamed at the overt invasion of their domestic privacy. "Look," he continued in a firmer tone, "You might say this has got nothing to do with me but I often sit in that pub when

Ralph's there. He's always insulting you and it... "

He paused for courage.

"It what, Len?' she replied, feeling equally ashamed.

"Well... it.." He drew breath and called out loudly: "It breaks my heart, Chris, it breaks my heart that anyone can treat you like this! He treats you like shit, Chris. Like shit! That's what he's doing! You know that, don't you? Eh?" He moved towards her, his stomach tightening as he spoke, the emotive tension all-consuming. He grabbed her by the arms, firmly, "You know that, don't you?" he repeated emphatically .

She broke down into a torrent of tears, her head falling onto his shoulder, her arms flung around his back. Lenny was moved. So moved, in fact, that he joined in the tearful outburst. It was as if a whole year's worth of heartache had finally been granted release.

They stood for a good five minutes simply weeping in a solid embrace.

He didn't know what to do. He wanted to kiss her. He wanted to exhibit all his repressed feelings. Now. He wanted to turn back the clock to their most joyous days.

His mind swept back to a hundred occasions when the skies seemed a permanent electric blue, when the birds incessantly warbled and when they were absolutely stuck to each other. Times when everything seemed to be in soft-focus.

He lifted his head, lifted hers and looked into her water-laden eyes. "You now I still love you, Giblet." he said softly.

She smiled with a sweet pathos, the affectionate name 'Giblet' bringing back her own fond memories.

"Yes, I know, Dribble," she replied, equally softly. He caressed her shaggy hair as if these personal terms were the password to authorised advances.

She grasped his hand and pulled it away from her hair. "Lenny, it wouldn't work. I can't give him up," she stated, quite unconvincingly, trying to balance the logic in her mind as she spoke.

"But why, Chris? I know I'm biased but honestly, I can't

understand why you stay with him. And it's not just me that thinks that: Bob and Reg both agree. They both think you're just being used."

There was a pause. She moved into the kitchen. The light came on, sending a dazzle through the house. She looked so beautiful, he thought. Even with blotchy mascara and sodden straggly hair, she looked gorgeous.

"Do you want a drink?" she asked quietly, wanting to expel those thoughts and occupy herself.

"What have you got?"

"Tea, coffee or lager. Oh, no, of course, you don't drink lager do you?"

"You remembered!" he responded in delight. "Tea would be fine, love." He entered the kitchen. "This washing up: do you want it done?"

"No, Len, just fish out a couple of mugs for me."

He rolled up his coat sleeves and dunked his bare arms into the bowl.

Lukewarm, curried water splashed over the edges; pieces of celery floated around like buoys. "What did you do with the curry?" he asked.

"It's in the bin, Len," she sighed "where all my meals end up."

He lifted up the lid, purely out of curiosity. A mound of coagulated sauce and rice was gradually shrouding other evidence of the night's dinner project: a brown stained milk carton, a brown stained curry sauce packet, damp curled onion skins and sticky limp celery leaves. A jagged tin with the word 'Ham' just visible was playing host to the more mobile dribbles and chunks.

He slopped around in the washing-up bowl and extracted a pair of mugs caked in a layer of yellow ochre sauce. He washed them thoroughly under the tap and handed them to Christine.

"Do you still insist on a teapot?" she asked.

"Don't worry, no, I can't be bothered these days, being single. By the time I've got halfway through a pot it's gone all stewed. It doesn't work if you're single, you know."

"You need a smaller pot. I bet you've still got that flowery one I bought you?"

He smiled in affirmation.

She flipped a teabag into each mug, poured on the boiling water and commenced prodding the bags with a stained spoon. The steam clung to the kitchen window and floated low, like a cool dawn mist, into the lounge. "I've even got fresh milk today. You're quite privileged," she grinned, reflecting on the disaster with the police's visit a week ago.

Lenny questioned her and she recounted the Archie Pond drama.

"So," she continued, "the police are satisfied that Archie's death was an accident - a heart attack brought on by stress and obesity, they reckon."

"What about Ralph? Does he accept the boss wasn't to blame?"

"No, not really. In fact, he's been getting more and more unbearable. He still insists that Clamp killed him and the Accountant is keeping quiet. He's still intimidating Clamp at every opportunity. I swear he'll lose his job if he carries on like that. And he's been drinking like there's no tomorrow. I hardly ever see him these days. He's down the pub whenever he's not working and when he does see me he's horrible."

"Seems to me you've been there before," suggested Leonard, referring to her unbearable ordeals with Pierre LePants several years ago. She shook her head, as if to resist such a prospect.

The pair stood in the kitchen for a further half an hour in deep conversation, Leonard frequently dropping heavy hints regarding his desire to reform their relationship. She was clearly confused. She rejected Lenny's submissions that Ralph's motive centred around her wealth, but he was sure that the more he could implant doubt, the greater the likelihood of their ultimate separation.

The front door clattered open and in swaggered Parmesan, belching furiously.

"Shit," whispered Leonard in panic.

Chris called: "All right, Ralph?" simultaneously unlocking and ushering Lenny out the back door and out of sight.

"No. I've just thrown up down my bloody work trousers," he spluttered. "You should eat, Ralph. You need to line your stomach when you're drinking"

"Line it with what?! I told you earlier, woman, I'm *not* eating your muck any more. I'd rather vomit every night than suffer your foul stuff!" he yelled crudely.

He slid off his shoes using his heels, not wishing to touch the sick-covered laces, unfastened his trousers and, balancing on one foot, tried to remove the particularly putrid trouser leg. He waivered, wobbled, teetered and tottered like an amateur surfer negotiating a tidal wave, and predictably toppled backwards.

Leonard witnessed the pathetic sight through a patch in the kitchen window's condensation. This repulsive, grown man struggling with outrageous incompetence, collapsing like a defenceless creature shot down by hunters. He watched Parmesan just lying there, spread-eagled in his twisted, encrusted trousers, totally insensible.

Leonard silently opened the back door: "Psst!" he whispered, beckoning Christine's attention. He extended his arm through the gap in the door and reached for hers.

"Chris, I can't bear to see you like this. I want you back. Please, please think about it," he impelled, squeezing her hand in desperation.

He released her and left.

chapter four
reg, reason and the raisin

Christine awoke, bright sunlight pouring into the bedroom. She shielded her eyes momentarily, thinking back at the previous night's events: Leonard's tempting pleas and Ralph's gruesome state.

She threw back the duvet and sat on the edge of the bed, wrapping her arms around her torso, shivering. She looked up and into the mirror on the wall. She studied herself: her blonde hair lacked its normal golden sheen, her eyes still bloated and smudged from her tearful episodes. Her cheekbones protruded, emphasising her drawn and saddened jowls. Her lips hung as if in mourning. Her eyes descended further: her neck red from worry sprouted out of her t-shirt, the shape and size of her breasts remaining secretive under the thick white cotton, save for the occasional contour punctuated by the harsh light on folds.

She arose, pointing her bare slim legs in the direction of two monstrous royal blue fluffy slippers and moved to the window. She tugged at one of the curtains, her eyes flinching as the light amplified. She stood, observing the movement in Church Lane below.

It was Sunday morning. A young lone cyclist was negotiating the thick snow, an orange sack of newspapers almost half his size challenging his equilibrium. She looked up at the blue and gold church clock glistening in the sun, its hands signalling the advent of the nine o'clock chimes. She imagined walking the route through the crisp snow to Leonard's terraced house. Down Church Lane past the church on the right and the shop on the left, into Sockwith Lane where the bus completed its route, and right into Cobblestone Street: the old brick public lavatories, the long row of hedges masking the recreation ground and pavilion, and then the humble red brick terraces with their tiny windows guarding the resident's cars, each respectfully placed outside their respective owners' homes.

She imagined knocking on the red door of number 4, still in just t-shirt and slippers and being dragged in passionately by Lenny.

She imagined him similarly dressed and smirked: it was the sort of thing he'd be pleased to participate in, whereas Parmesan had become singularly grim and introverted.

Then it struck her that Ralph must still be downstairs unconscious, doubtlessly in the exact spot he fell. She decided to get dressed before facing him, not wishing to arouse him in her semi-naked state.

Descending the stairs quietly and carefully, she peeped into the lounge. He was, indeed, still sited on the floor. His pale carcass lay static. His trousers were all the more twisted, ruffled between his knees and ankles, valleys in the fabric acting as receptacles for the crisped vomit. His scrawny thighs and baggy Y-fronts looked like they'd been sculptured out of grey alabaster. She shuddered in revulsion and continued to inwardly question her partnership with this being. Or was he a being? She suddenly realised he could be dead, such was his cataleptic state. She moved nearer, knelt by his side and studied his jacket-covered chest for signs of life. There was a sudden, wild grunt from the man. His whole body tremored. Christine almost somersaulted in fright. His sudden pulsation lapsed back to immediate comatose.

She couldn't have faced removing his foul clothes last night but now, her palpitations subsiding, knew she had to perform the hideous task before he awoke; to negate further verbal abuse, more than out of duty. She knelt once more, at his feet this time, and slowly collected his trousers by grasping at pieces devoid of rotten regurgitant discharge. His legs were cold, hard and heavy.

She finally gathered the entire pair of trousers, hooking at the back pockets, scrunching them up and transporting them quickly and directly into the washing machine.

She returned to the lounge and looked once more at him:

red socks, one with a big toe glowing through an old tear; those spindly legs with cold hairs erect, the dishevelled pair of lumpy grey underpants; the thick black coat, a fixture all year round except in the hottest of weather, topped by his palid face and thick ruffled chunk of hair.

Her repulsion turned to pity. She reflected on his life for a few minutes: the tragedy of his late disabled father, a man that had relinquished his status as a vicar to marry Ralph's mother, out of moral responsibility when Ralph was twelve after the scandal of an illegitimate son had surfaced. His invalidity had been caused a few years previous to the wedding when, during a turbulent sermon on ethical adherence, he'd gesticulated and girated so dramatically, that he'd fallen from the pulpit and broken his back, causing permanent paralysis.

Ralph had dearly loved his father, regardless of the little time they were given together through his childhood. The Reverend Ron Parmesan had been devoted to his new wife, Muriel, until he discovered that she was having a rampant affair with an aristocrat in the neighbouring parish, one Major Plankton Bleach-Parsley. One day she'd simply packed her suitcases and left home to cohabit with this rich old eccentric. Ralph's father died four years ago after a long illness, initiated apparently by the devastation of their separation. Perhaps that's why Ralph had become so cold-hearted and aggressive - a despairing rebellion against his parental inefficaciousness, she philosophised. And perhaps now Ralph is subconsciously mirroring his mother's actions by trying to marry into money?

Ralph seldom received or sent any communication to his mother. He treated her relationship with the Major with utter contempt. He'd receive the obligatory birthday and Christmas card, simply signed *Mum and Plankton* and he'd occasionally, reluctantly reciprocate.

Christine went to the cupboard under the staircase and returned with an old greatcoat. She placed it over his bottom half and left the room.

She washed, made up her face, put on her coat, suede boots and left the house.

The air was brisk and fresh, odd flutters of snow dropping from overladen rooftops and gutters. The church bells were clanging their announcement that the Service was due to commence. Colourful figures were moving unidirectionally to St Barnaby's, randomly slipping and sliding in the snow.

She arrived at the general store, an all-purpose retail establishment, housing abbreviated versions of a post office, newsagent, tobacconist, chemist and grocer's. The doorbell clanged in discord with the old church bells.

"Hi, Chris, how's you?" greeted Lenny's friend, Reg Book.

"Oh, Okay, thanks", she replied politely. "Roped in to working today, then?"

"Yeah. I don't mind. At least it's only a trip downstairs," Reg commented. As Sub-Postmaster, he had the privilege of living in a flat above the shop. Reg was a pleasant bloke, nearing 30 years old but with a childish, playful streak which made him amiable to most of the village community.

"Anything in particular you want, Chris?' he enquired, noticing her drift aimlessly round the shelves.

"Err, I don't know, really. I just needed to get out the house, if you know what I mean..."

"Oh. Like that is it?" he said sympathetically. "Still having problems then?" She didn't mind him asking. He was a friend who shared most of her problematic challenges with genuine concern. Their relationship had always been platonic. She considered him a funny, cuddly sort of chap: the sort to whom you could bare your soul in the most vulnerable situation, with the security of a warm, understanding response. He was, indeed, cuddly. He had a rotundness of jollity and fulfilment rather than gluttony. Every feature, every limb appeared to be round, from his fingers to his curly hair.

"Lenny was really wound up last night," he commented.

"Was he?" she responded with an innocent pretence. "What about?" She was inspecting a tin of pilchards, turning it every which way, nervously.

"We heard Ralph on the phone in the Plank. You know: when he was giving you earache."

"Oh, that," she sighed.

"Yes," Reg continued, "Len was all for smacking Ralph one. We had to drag him out the pub."

"Lenny would never hit anyone!" retorted Christine in defence.

"He was going to do it, I swear. I've never seen him so angry. Bob and I really thought he was going to lay into him. It would have been an almighty scrap. Ralph had been firing nasty comments all night and when Lenny heard him on the phone to you... well!"

She walked up to the counter guarded by Reg and picked up a packet of Fisherman's Friends, again inspecting them. Still looking down she said in a soft voice, "Len's still serious about me, isn't he?"

"Yes," Reg replied with resignation. "I'm afraid he is. It was New Year's Eve you dropped him wasn't it? God, that's virtually a year ago..."

"Mmm," she grunted with a hint of regret.

They both remembered the occasion clearly: it was early on at a New Year's Eve Party in the village pavilion. As usual, Leonard had been smothering her with charm, affection and kisses, to the point where his continual amorous suffocation had finally become intolerable.

"You'd really had enough of him, hadn't you?!" Reg reflected, grinning. "I remember you screaming at him in the middle of the dance floor when he objected to you dancing with Ginny! It's not even as if Ginny's a bloke! That really was the last straw, wasn't it?" he laughed.

Christine looked up at Reg's globe-like face, his little round eyes and sparkling white teeth.

Chris grinned for a second and then looked back down at the packet she was still molesting, her expression straightening.

"You know what, Reg?" she questioned, soberly.

"What?" he replied, stifling his laugh.

"Looking back on it, I think I'd rather be loved and smothered rotten than..."

"I know what you're saying. He'd have you back today if he could..."

"I'm so scared. I've never told anyone this but... I really am scared of Ralph."

She replaced the packet and lightly dragged her forefinger over four rows of confectionery, the chocolate bars vibrating.

"The thing is, Chris," he said authoritatively, leaning forward, his arms resting on the till, "You've got to live your life the way *you* want to. That's what I do. If people get up my nose, I just think 'cobblers to them' and carry on doing my own thing."

He paused, seeking some profound statement of persuasion. "I mean, what's the point in you living your life in misery? And Ralph can't be that happy either. All right, he's got you, the most sought after girl in Larynx, but from what I see of him, he's as miserable as a... as a bullock without bollocks!" he grinned proudly.

She snorted with amusement at his ridiculous analogy.

"I mean," he continued, "can you see yourself with Ralph in five or six years' time? What will you be doing? Will you be happy?"

"No, I can't," was her instant response. "In fact, I can't see us in a month, let alone years..." .

"Well there you are then," he concluded, straightening himself and wringing his hands together as if in triumph.

He thought further and added: "Dare I say this but you might not see yourself with Lenny *either*. It may be that you're better off unattached for a while. You don't *have* to have a bloke all the time, you know . But only *you* can decide what's best."

"Yes," she said, her tone intimating sadness, triggered by the sudden realisation that she may end up a spinster.

"Why don't you have a proper, serious talk with Ralph - get it all out in the open - how you feel and find out how *he* feels... and maybe do the same with Lenny, if necessary... But you won't be able to do anything until you find out where you really stand, will you? And the worst thing would be for you to walk out on Ralph without any warning. He'd go stark-raving bonkers!"

"Yes," she said, looking up at him again. "I'm going to go and have a really serious think."

"A *positive* think!" Reg stressed, punching the air with his fist, with motivation.

"Yes!" she replied, cheering up. "A positive think!"

She turned away, thanking him.

" Any time! You know where Agony Aunt Reg is, whenever you need me. Take care."

She trudged her way the few hundred yards back home.

Ralph's grey underpants, red socks and cream woollen jumper marked the place where he'd earlier rested. She tutted, collected the smelly clothes and thrust them into the machine to accompany his trousers. She slammed the machine door, poured an excessive heap of powder into its drawer, rotated a couple of knobs and watched as the stale clothing began their rough, torrid ride to cleanliness.

"Ralph?" she called, walking towards the stairs. Perhaps he'd gone to bed? She popped her head briefly round each door.

"Well, the pubs aren't open yet," she pondered.

She walked around the village and ended up at the Larynx Olde Tea Shoppe where she helped out, open Sunday mornings to capture the spiritual congregation, before and after worship.

"Hi, Ginny," Chris greeted the owner.

"Hello. What brings you here today?" questioned Virginia Chisel, placing a few more cream buns in the glass display case on the counter.

"I'm looking for Ralph, actually. He's gone out and I don't know where..."

"Perhaps he's in the pub?"

"No - they don't open until noon on Sundays."

She watched as Virginia artistically rearranged the fresh cakes and sandwiches in the cabinet. Ginny cared hugely about her shop. Everything was spotlessly clean and fresh. Insects daren't invade these premises, such were the number of ultra-violet contraptions mounted on every wall and bug destruction sprays concealed behind plotted plants in every corner.

Ginny was a likeable woman, a few years older than Chris; Christine's only real girlfriend. She was tall and lanky with a pale, freckly face and lengthy ginger hair that was wound and fixed up during work like a haystack with an array of pins, clips and brackets. She always wore immense earrings: ornamental baubles that would suit the largest of Christmas trees. They wobbled excitedly with the slightest twinge, her earlobes following their motion like two hinges supporting a child's swing. Her eyes were large and chestnut brown, housed amongst long eyelashes and topped by the thinnest eyebrow line.

She looked up as the teashop door opened, gesturing to Chris. It was Ralph.

He parked himself at a small round table by the window and unfolded his Sunday paper, the supplement and loose inserts dropping onto the floor. He reached down, Christine catching his eye as his head descended.

"Oh, hello," he greeted quietly.

"Hi, Ralph..." She pulled back the other chair and sat, arms folded leaning towards him. "How are you? Are you okay now?"

"Yeah," he replied flickering his eyes at her briefly from above the News of the World. She glanced at the headline, thick and bold on the front cover: *"QUEEN MUM GUZZLES GALLON OF GUINNESS - EXCLUSIVE".*

"Ralph," she continued.

"What?" he muttered, shielded by his paper.

"We need to talk."

"Do we?" came his disinterested response.

"Yes... look..." She reached out and curled her fingers round his wrist, pulling the paper away from his face. "Look, Ralph... how about going to the Raisin for lunch, a drink and a natter? I think we ought to sort things out."

"Lunch and a drink?" he repeated, puzzled. "Mmm... " He

folded the paper and placed it on his lap. He sat upright, looking at her inquisitively. "You want to buy me lunch at the Blunt Raisin and a few pints?" he repeated ensuring a clear interpretation of her proposal.

"That's right."

"All right. What's the time?"

She looked up at the round pink clock above Ginny's head. "Quarter to twelve."

"Oh," he said, disappointed.

"Shall we have a coffee and then we'll stroll round at twelve?"

"Yeah. Get us a black one."

Christine walked up to the counter. "A black coffee and I'll have a cappuccino, please Ginny. Do you want me to make them?"

"No, its okay. Go and sit down and I'll bring them over," replied Ginny sweetly.

Clouds of steam rose to the ceiling and hisses spat from the hot water tap, like a steam train responding to the whistle. Cups and saucers rattled, teaspoons clinked.

"Here," Ginny presented them with the tray bearing two crisp white bone china cups. She bent down to the table, her earrings inches away from the cups' brims.

"Thanks," Chris replied, smiling. She placed Ralph's black coffee between his arms and slid her cappuccino across the chequered pink tablecloth, the chocolate crumbs rocking peacefully on the surface, some clinging to the edges.

They sat for ten minutes hardly speaking. She watched him staring out the window, occasionally straining his head to see the church clock. He sipped his coffee almost unknowingly, his concentration clearly devoted to the hands meeting twelve and the signal to admit alcohol.

"Come on, let's go!" He jumped up, his chair scraping back on the linoleum. He slapped his newspaper into the palm of his hand with a 'smack' like the firing of a starting pistol and he strode out of the café with excited purpose. Chris followed behind, pointing to a pound coin she'd left on the table. Virginia nodded and waved.

The Blunt Raisin was an old rickety pub, dimly lit, mainly catering for the middle-aged and older generations, attracting diners from a good ten mile radius. They served fine meals in the mezzanine restaurant and prided themselves on the calm, restful ambience, accentuated by soft sofas and armchairs, a large open fire and smart, smiling waiters and waitresses.

The landlord's face dropped when Ralph entered, lifting slightly when he realised he was in Christine's company.

"Good afternoon, Mr Parmesan, Miss Ribcage," nodded the landlord formally, his small lips shadowed under a precipice of thick black moustache. "What can I get you to drink?"

"A Pils for me," snapped Ralph, rocking on the bar in excitement. "Bottle or draught, sir?" enquired the landlord.

"That." Ralph pointed to a small sombre tap, the absolute contrast to the Crusts architectural eyesore in the Grinning Plank. "It's the nearest they've got here to Crusts," he explained to his girlfriend, as if it were a sacrifice.

"And I'll have a Malibu with orange juice, please, Jim."

"Right you are." He proceeded to efficiently fill their glasses. "Three pound twenty, please."

"Can I put it on a tab? We're going to eat."

"Of course, Madam," he responded, accepting her Visa card.

"Would you like a table, Madam?" he asked, reaching for a pair of leather-look menus.

"Yes. In about half an hour?"

"Fine," he agreed.

The couple sunk into an old, blue-grey sofa facing the fire, placing their drinks on a glowing oak coffee table. Ralph's glass was almost empty. Chris wondered for a second whether he must have spilt it: she hadn't noticed him take a single swig.

"Good stuff, that," he commented, gesticulating at the frothy glass. "Not as good as Crusts but not bad."

"Ralph," she began, thinking and speaking slowly and

clearly. "I think we ought to talk."

"We are. Do you want another?" he said, pushing himself up out of the soft cushion, glass in hand.

"No, not yet." She grabbed his coat sleeve, preventing him from moving away. "Sit down, Ralph "

"Hang on, let me just get another pint!" he said quickly, tugging his arm away as if she was threatening his enjoyment.

He came back seconds later with his second drink, slurping it down to the half pint mark.

"Ralph, we need to talk about *us"* she emphasised. "Can you leave your drink for a minute and listen, please."

He slumped right back, glass in hand and stretched his feet under the table in submission.

"Look, Ralph," she continued, "these last few weeks have been pretty unbearable for both of us, haven't they?" she started bravely, her eyes frequently glancing up at couples entering, ordering and sitting. She kept her voice low. Ralph sat perfectly still, save for the odd twitch of fingers on glass, resisting the urge to swallow the lot in one gulp.

"We've had an awful time. I've hardly seen you and when I have it's been around midnight, out of control, in a mess and, well, to be honest, really quite nasty," she said reserving a selection of more caustic adjectives for later, if the need arose.

Ralph opened his mouth, preparing to announce his defence. Christine hastily continued. "I know Archie's death was awful and I know my cooking's awful. But does that really justify the way you treat me?" She was wrapping her right arm round his left, comforting him as she spoke, trying to soften the blow of her words.

"I want you to talk to me, Ralph. I want us to get everything off our chests so we know where we stand and where we go from here."

It was now her turn to sit in silence. She'd released her carefully worded preamble and now awaited the response.

He sighed, still twitching his glass, and rambled a string of "Umms" and "Errs" whilst shaping his reply, his normal arrogance superseded by a rare humility. Christine continued to wait patiently for a coherent reply. The restaurant was getting busier, young staff flitting around preparing tables and waiting on customers.

"I know I've been crap," Ralph admitted at last, surrendering unreservedly. "In fact, if the truth be known, I've probably behaved like this for much longer than a few weeks. The thing is," he continued, "I don't really know what's happening to me. My job's been under threat. In fact, Clamp has already sacked me..."

"Sacked you?" came Christine in surprise, sitting up.

"Yes, last week - but he's keeping me on," he continued.

"What do you mean?"

"He got me in his office last week. He said that he'd had enough of me coming in to work 'smelling of booze and unwashed'. Also he said he'd had enough of my sniping about him being responsible for Archie's death." Ralph was getting agitated. "God, I hate that man," he muttered under his breath, finally succumbing to the remainder of his lager. "But he's keeping me on," he said indignantly, swirling the base of the pint glass. "I threatened him with the papers. I told him that I'd expose his sordid past at the factory."

"What sordid past?" questioned Chris with a shocked concern.

"I don't know," he replied, grinning. "I was calling his bluff. But when I mentioned it, Clamp's face went as white as a sheet! He's got something to hide. I hit a raw nerve. Clamp didn't even question me. He just looked stunned: I've got him round my little finger now!" He clenched his fist victoriously. "He's keeping me on, with a pay rise, and he's now promised I'll be the first to drive one of the new buses. He knows he's got to keep me sweet." He touched her shoulder, rising once again. "Another drink now?" he smiled.

"Err... yes, okay," she replied. She was worried, really worried. What was Ralph getting tangled up in?

A young girl in black and white who had been hovering

nearby, approached her. "Excuse me. Sorry to interrupt but your table's ready now. Table number 5."

"Oh, thanks" replied Chris, getting up, taking her drink from Ralph as he returned from the bar. They walked up the steps and the girl gestured to their allocated table. They handed their coats to the waitress and sat opposite each other. The girl handed them two more menus.

"What shall we have then?"

"Anything you want, Ralph," she replied generously.

His eyes lit up at the prospect of complete freedom of choice from the four pages of beautifully described dishes.

The girl returned. "Are you ready to order?"

"Yeah." Ralph excitedly listed his selection: "Err Deep Fried Garlic Mushrooms... err can I have them with some Thousand Island stuff, please?"

"If that's what you want, sir," smiled the waitress, slightly bemused.

"And," he continued, his finger running down the next page to the appropriate title, "Your 22 ounce sirloin steak with chips, peas and jacket potato... "

"Yes... " prompted the waitress, scribbling furiously and frowning. "And how would you like your steak done, sir?"

"Done? Err..," he floundered.

"Rare, Medium or Well, Sir?"

He glared at Christine for enlightenment. She silently mouthed the words "Well Done" to him across the table.

"Err, Well Done," he muttered, hoping he'd got it right.

"I'll have the Prawn Surprise, and the Tagliatelli Ameritriciana, please," Chris requested, with perfect pronunciation. She handed the menu to the girl and Ralph did the same.

A man in black and white arrived with a basket of bread rolls.

"Rolls?" he offered, extending the basket close to Ralph's face.

"Oh, thanks," Ralph said, taking the basket and entire

contents from the man and placing it in front of him, delighted by their apparent generosity. He started rummaging through them for his first choice of roll: white, brown, soft, crusty, wholemeal, round, twirly, long like for hot dogs....?

The man stood there aghast.

"Ralphy," Chris whispered, "You're meant to take one or two and give the rest back to the waiter."

"Oh." His face turned scarlet, picked out a hurried selection of three rolls and thrust the basket back at the man. The man revolved and disappeared down the steps, making no attempt to serve Christine.

The waitress brought their food with impressive efficiency. The couple sat eating, drinking and politely talking, Chris occasionally correcting slips in Ralph's etiquette.

Having completed their main course, Christine raised the subject of Arbuthnot Clamp and Ralph's threats once more. She wanted to resolve her concerns.

"Don't worry about it," urged Parmesan, sitting back, relaxed and rubbing his stomach. "He thinks I know something dodgy about him when he was at Griswald's Pie Factory and he doesn't want word getting out. He takes me dead seriously. He won't risk upsetting me in any way. He's obviously got a lot to lose."

She remained worried but knew that pursuit of this matter was futile.

"What about us, though, Ralph?" she continued. "We haven't really got a relationship any more, have we? You do your thing and I do mine."

"That's how we wanted it from the start," he explained, "That's what we agreed!"

"Yes but we didn't agree you'd come home after closing time every night half cut, hurling abuse at me."

"Are you asking me to stop drinking?" he asked forcefully, the prospect of which would be disastrous.

"No, I'm not, Ralph. If you want to drink, then carry on. What I'm questioning is whether you really want *me* any more?

It's obvious you want the pub and the buses. But as I see it, I come right down your list."

Ralph clammed up for a moment and started twisting his soiled serviette. "Perhaps that's it. Perhaps you're right," he admitted quietly. "Perhaps we should call off the wedding and split."

"Is that what you want?" she asked, softly reaching for his hand.

"I don't know." He pondered, ruffling his temple, weighing up the pros and cons. "What do *you* want?" he asked with unprecedented diplomacy.

"I'm not sure either, Ralph. But I do know that we can't go on the way we are. Either we make changes to help each other or we call it a day."

"Right," he muttered, knowing that only one of these alternatives was realistic.

"What about France?" he asked.

"France?"

"Yeah, its the Village's Christmas trip on Tuesday. We were going to get loads of booze and stuff in, remember? I wanted to get my baguettes and cheeses. I wanted to go to France, come back, go down the Grinning Plank until closing time, go home and stuff my face with bread and cheese. I've been looking forward to that," he said sorrowfully.

"Let's do it then. There's no reason why even if we split up, we can't still go to odd places together and have a laugh. I'd forgotten all about that trip. No, let's do it, let's have a good time!" she said, smacking his hand reassuringly. "Oh, that reminds me, I'm supposed to be staying at Ginny's Tuesday night: I was going to go into Sockwith with her once we'd got back from France."

"All right," he exclaimed cheerily. "Do it then!"

It seemed like they'd reached their decision: to split up but remain on good terms.

Things weren't finalised by any means. Christine's living accommodation would need reviewing, wedding arrangements cancelled, possessions fairly shared and so on. But she was relieved that the most painful and potentially explosive part had passed without incident.

"Ironic, really" he muttered pensively. "This is the first meal we've had together for ages and it's probably our last. Another drink?"

chapter five
the french revelation

Chris and Ralph strolled home, arm-in-arm. They had made their peace and were now the best of friends. As they passed the general store, Leonard Mantlepiece came out of the doorway. The pair continued on their way, Leonard standing watching, witnessing their closeness. He darted back into the shop.

"Reg?"

"Yeah?"

"What's going on there?" he questioned, pointing out the window.

"What do you mean?" Reg asked.

"Chris and Parmesan: they're arm-in-arm! They look all loved-up! What's going on?"

"I suppose they've made up," reasoned Reg. "She was saying this morning that she wanted to sort things out, one way or the other."

"Well it certainly looks like they've patched things up!" Leonard slammed his hands on the counter in frustration. "I thought it was over! I thought she was going to come back to me!"

"Calm down! You *don't know* what's happened, do you? Why don't you go and see her later and ask her?"

"What's the point?! Its obvious, isn't it?!" He stormed out of the shop, the bell above the door swinging and clattering in anger.

He sat on the bench in the square watching the snow slowly melt around him.

The crisp scrunching underfeet had turned to damp squelching. Cars were leaving The Blunt Raisin car park behind him and sploshing their way back to the neighbouring villages. He reached into his jacket pocket, flipped open a pack of cigarettes, pulled one out, inserted it between his cold lips, lighting it between his shielding hands.

He sat hunched, elbows on knees, gently rocking back and forth. The cigarette smoke mingled with the steam from his breath in the dense, misty wintry air.

A tall girl moved in front of him and stopped. "Hi, Len. Are you all right?"

It was Ginny. She'd just closed the Tea Shoppe and was twirling the large bunch of keys around her stripy woollen-gloved fingers. He looked up at her, a plump knitted hat concealing her towering red hair, her earrings stroking her cheeks as she looked down at him.

"What's going on with Chris?" he asked, pleading for reason.

"Don't know, really," she replied calmly, brushing the wet from the bench with her gloves and sitting, caressing her keys.

"I've just seen them strolling arm-in-arm down the road there - as if they're madly in love ... I can't believe it.. not after what's happened."

"I really don't know. But there's no point getting all worked up. Be patient. You never know, you may have misread it."

"Yeh, yeh, yeh. I doubt that very much! I'm going home." He got up, flicking away the remains of his cigarette. Ginny called after him: "Are you still going to France with us on Tuesday?"

He turned. "Yes, I'll be there, even if I have to put up with *them* together."

That evening, the Grinning Plank played host once more to Ralph, Leonard, Reg and Bob. Ralph was predictably perched at the bar with his personalised crystal tankard. The trio sat at their usual table, Lenny's friends making every effort to lighten his mood, attempting to generate some excitement over the forthcoming day trip to France. This was a yearly exercise, organised by Bob through the Sockwith Minibus Hire Company for the locals craving their festive stocks of duty free drink, tobacco and food. Bob worked for the Company as part of the booking office team, occupied in the approach to Christmas by organising these popular trips to the French ports, with most of the surrounding villages participating.

"We'll have a laugh, Len!" encouraged Bob. "We always do, mate! And this year will be even better because we arrive home around six so we'll still have time for the pub when we get back!"

Christine came in, a rare sight in the evenings. She walked up to Ralph and ordered them both a drink from Bert. Reg called her over.

"Hi, chaps," greeted Chris, smiling. "Hi, Len..."

Lenny grunted, still bitter over his earlier conclusions. She sat next to Bob mouthing "What's wrong with him?" Bob shook his head as if to negate any progress on that subject and mouthed back "I'll tell you later."

Leonard just sat, tapping, turning and twisting his packet of Benson and Hedges.

"Are you still going on Tuesday, Chris?" asked Bob, breaking the silence.

"To Calais? Oh most certainly," replied Christine. "I'm just going for the day out, really - but Ralph's going to stock up with lager, as you might expect," she said, rolling her eyes.

"We're all coming down here when we get back, just to round off a good day out," added Reg. "Would you like to join us?"

"Oh, no, I can't, I'm afraid. I'm going into Sockwith with Ginny and stopping over at her house."

"Oh, never mind," continued Reg, slurping his Old Blagger.

"I know Ralph's coming down here afterwards. He was saying earlier that he's going to get loads of french bread and cheese and devour it after closing time back at home," she explained, still rolling her eyes.

Leonard grunted again. How dare she talk about *him,* he thought. How insensitive. He got up.

"I'm feeling ill. I'll see you tomorrow, I suppose," he

mumbled and left.

"What's wrong with him?" asked Christine, disturbed.

"He's well fed up," explained Reg quietly, not wishing Ralph to hear. "He saw you with Ralph this afternoon when you passed the shop. He says you were arm-in-arm. He got quite rattled seeing you two so close."

Christine tutted and shook her head. "We've decided to split up. We were walking together more out of mutual relief than affection or anything."

"Split up... have you?" Bob responded. "Lenny ought to know. He's so depressed, you know."

"Well, I don't know what I'm going to do yet, Bob," explained Chris. "I haven't decided whether to get back with Len or just spend some time by myself. Whatever, though, it's definitely over between Ralph and I."

"How did he take it?" enquired Reg, recalling his advice in the shop earlier. "He was amazingly fine. He *admitted* it wasn't working out. It was quite easy, really!"

"Told you so!" said Reg, delighted that she had profited from his consultation.

"Don't say anything to Lenny yet," she requested. "I'd like to talk to him myself once I've thought things through. I'll try and grab him tomorrow. It'll be better if I explain things to him."

"Okay," the two lads concurred.

An argument at the bar was gaining momentum. Christine looked round to see Ralph standing, cursing a man. The man was soaked in beer, his hair dripping over his foreign face. The victim was Pierre LePants.

Pierre, a largely-built man in his early thirties was yelling French obscenities back at Parmesan, gesticulating wildly. Pierre was once Christine's lover, preceding her relationship with Leonard. He'd been most violent to her. Ralph was quite gentle by comparison.

His long, permed hair flapped and dripped around his head like a wedge of aggravated seaweed, whilst he motioned angrily at Parmesan.

Chris got up, annoyed that Ralph's temperament had deteriorated yet again. She grabbed Ralph's shoulder tightly.

"What the hell's going on?" she demanded sternly.

"It's this French bastard. He couldn't take a joke and now his spitting his filthy onion breath at me!"

"Oh, calm down, the pair of you!" she shouted, slapping them both simultaneously with frustration.

The Frenchman spoke: "He made some filthy pig joke about how the French could not possibly be regarded as good lovers," he explained, his English displaying only the mereist hint of French origin. "He was taking the piss, how you could have possibly enjoyed making love with me," he continued. "I say to him, this stinking alcoholic arseface..." pointing and waving his fingers within millimetres of Ralph's nose, "If he is so good, why is he always getting pissed? Why doesn't he care for you the way I cared for you?"

"Care?" laughed Ralph. *"When did you ever care for her? You just beat her. You were a bastard!"*

He pushed LePants against the bar, clenching his fists in preparation for an almighty fight. Both these lads were hot-tempered, pugnacious and irrational.

"What the hell are you both fighting for?" Chris screamed again. "Neither of you have got me! You're both in the past. I really don't care for either of you! Now just shut up and grow up!!" Again she was pushing them, infuriated at the pointless row: one based solely on male pride.

They continued, ignoring Christine's pleas for peace. She stormed out.

"At least I didn't get her pregnant, you stinking git!" whispered Ralph into the Frenchman's damp ear. This tactic, he calculated, would close the entire argument down without the need for public advertisement.

"What? How do you know about that?" Pierre reacted, equally quietly, shocked that anyone should know his shameful secret. His mouth almost on Ralph's nose, spat garlic fumes into his orifices.

"Don't you ever ever ever.." (he prodded Ralph three times firmly in the chest) " ... mention that again, do you hear?"

"I tell you what..." remonstrated Parmesan, this time pushing his face into Pierre's, "if you ever mess with me again, the whole village will know about it, including your wife. Get the message, you murderous French git?!" He prodded him back.

"Don't even think about it, filthy pig," spat back Pierre.

The prodding continued, scrawny Ralph equalling the Rugby player-shaped foreigner. In fact Pierre had lived in this country since he was sent to an English University over ten years ago. He looked French, his voice was flavoured with it (as was his breath) but most people in Larynx treated him like one of the locals.

"I'm warning you, Pants!" called Ralph, carrying on the duel, "One more word *ever* to me and I'm going to your missus, understand?"

Ralph's threats referred back to a terrifyingly traumatic time four years back when Pierre and Chris lived together. She'd accidentally got pregnant by him and decided to keep the baby. One night, in one of his physical outrages, he punched and kicked her repeatedly, fully intending to destroy the foetus. He had no desire for a child and this seemed the simplest solution for one who exploited his rampant temper so frequently. Nobody was meant to know except, of course, Christine. It was this incident that had finally split them up. She was shattered for months after this hideous assault and it was Lenny who had devoted the most care and attention to her. The police were never involved due to Christine's fear of repercussions.

LePants had softened considerably over the years, sincerely regretful over the maltreatment of Christine Ribcage. He was bereft of a girlfriend for two years following this series of physical violations, his reputation sorely damaged.

He'd met his future wife in Sockwith and mostly kept her away from Larynx until the village had generally granted him forgiveness and accepted him as a reformed character. His marriage a few months back to Pandora was in itself a statement of his new-found stability and calm nature. Their relationship was as good as any.

It was obvious that Pierre now felt seriously threatened by Ralph's knowledge of his regretable past.

"I kill you! I swear I kill you if ever you mention this to *anyone!*" Pierre screamed, poking his index finger half up Ralph's nose. He moved to the door still shouting "I kill you, I kill you!"

As the door slammed, Ralph called out "You wait and see, shitface!"

The pub hushed into silence. Ralph looked round at everyone and chuckled, dribbling lager down his chin.

chapter six
threats and settlements

Leonard Mantlepiece had a disturbed night with little sleep. His innards felt taut from worry and frustration.

At 6:30am on Monday he telephoned his manager, leaving a message on his answer machine.

"Hi, Geoff, it's Leonard. Sorry to call you so early but I'm feeling really rough. I've got a stomach upset and won't be able to come in. I thought I'd ring you now as I'm going to try to get to the doctor's first thing."

Leonard worked for the Sockwith Insurance Bureau, studying domestic claims for motor and household losses. He'd worked there for five years and was doing well, most claims relying on his individual judgement before being given onward authorisation to the insurers themselves.

There were many claims that he'd photocopied for their illiteracy and stupidity which he had framed across his bedroom walls.

"I was driving along the Canal Ring Road at 8:00pm," one read, *"following a motorcycle delivering pizzas. The bike went over a pothole and a pizza loosened itself from its bungees. I tried to avoid it as it approached but it happened so fast. The pizza flew out of its box and hit my windscreen with force. The mess made by the cheese, pepperoni and anchovy topping totally obscured my vision and I crashed into a shop window. My car was written off."*

A second, in scrawly handwriting had the following description: *"My yungist sun, age 4 made me set fire to our lownge. My sun's name is Dillon. He had picked up my fag from the ashtray while I was hooovering. He then tripped on the hooover wire, splashing my glass of brandy over the curtens, dropping my fag onto the windowlege. I think that the fag must have started to make the kurtens burn and the brandy made it worse. By the time I had turned round from hooovering, the other bit of the roome was in flames and we had to get out quick."*

And a third: *"I was watching Match of the Day when my wife came in with a big jug of water to water the plants. She started watering the cheeseplant in its pot on the telly and when Spurs scored, I screamed and clapped, causing her to jump, splashing water into the vents on the back of the telly and it exploded. Spurs apparently won 3-nil. I wish to claim for a new telly, video and cheeseplant. Can I also claim for a new wife?"*

Ralph Parmesan, ready for another day on the buses, was finishing his cup of coffee as Christine came down from the bedroom in her nightgown.

"Right, I'm off. I'll see you tonight, Chris."

"Okay. Are you going straight to the pub after work?"

"Yeah, probably," he answered.

"It's just that we ought to spend some time sorting out when I should leave and what things I can take with me, you know. Shall I meet you in there?"

"Yes, all right. Come down any time after six."

"And don't forget we've got an early start tomorrow, so you ought to have an early night," referring to the village day trip to Calais.

"Right. Bye."

Ralph caught the 7:40 bus into Sockwith. He collected his ticket machine and cash bag. He walked proudly to his black number 47 bus, the doors flapped open and he climbed into his seat, arranging his things ready for the rush hour onslaught. An envelope perched above the steering wheel, addressed to *R Parmesan.* He opened it. It was a typewritten letter on SCT headed paper.

Ralph, I would appreciate you meeting me in my office after today's shift (Monday) to discuss private matters between us. I expect to see you at 5:00pm. A Clamp, Chief Executive.

Ralph wondered whether he'd been found out by Clamp; whether Clamp had realised that he'd been calling his bluff over the supposed Griswald's Pie Scandal. He spent the morning weighing up how to increase his ammunition against Clamp, to maintain the credibility of his threats. He wanted to keep his job and payrise at any cost.

At the terminus at the far end of his route he leapt out of the bus, ran into a Newsagents and bought the last issue of the Sockwith Weekly News. He dashed into a telephone box. He rang the newsroom number.

"Yeah, hello. Newsroom? I'd like to arrange a meeting with one of your journalists. I have a piece of news that will make headlines, not just for you but probably for the national papers as well."

"Your name, sir?"

"I'd rather not say."

"Can you tell me the story in brief so that we know whether it is really worth pursuing?"

"Afraid not... let's just say it's regarding a Chief Executive of one of Sockwith's well-known businesses and his shocking past in a factory."

"Oh yes?" came the response, showing slightly more interest.

"Look," continued Parmesan hurriedly. He had an eye kept on his bus parked a few yards away, a small queue beginning to form looking anxiously around for the driver. "Can we just fix up a time, say Wednesday evening in the Gum and Grommet in The High Street?"

"All right, sir. How will I know you?"

"I'll tell Barney the landlord that I'm expecting you, so ask him and he'll point me out. Say seven o'clock in the Gum and Grommet then?"

"All right. But I hope you're not wasting our time... "

"You wait. You won't regret it! Bye." Parmesan clattered the phone down, hopped apologetically to the bus and continued his work. He was delighted with his inspired idea. By phoning the papers and arranging a meeting, he was all the more armed for his meeting with Clamp later. Whilst he didn't have a *story* to tell the papers, at the least, if it came to it, he could name Arbuthnot Clamp and the fact an unexposed scandal clearly existed. His preference was to avoid any publicity: his job depended on maintaining the current equilibrium with Clamp and, particularly with his impending separation from Christine, his independent financial stability was all the more crucial.

Meanwhile, Christine was trying to reach Leonard. She wanted to explain the previous day's agreement between Ralph and herself. She'd thought long and hard about her own future. Should she move back in with Lenny? That would give her a roof over her head and the love and warmth that seemed to be exclusively offered by him. But would the relationship become unbearably stifling once more? If, on the other hand, she decided to go her own way, setting up her own home and singular existence, at least temporarily, would she be able to cope? She had lived and catered for men for so many years that the prospect of a quiet, self-focussed existence seemed far less attractive. The third option was to move back to her family. Her mother, father and two younger brothers all lived in the Midlands. They had moved there from Larynx during the early stages of her relationship with Pierre LePants. Her father had been offered a job in hotel management for one of the large conference hotels which included free accommodation for the entire family and improved their standard of living considerably.

Chris had always vowed to remain in Larynx. Her competition win gave her more reason to remain independent. In reality, she had spent so long away from her family that returning would be an unbearable culture shock.

Her decision had finally been made by lunchtime: to return to Leonard, with a few conditions, the major one pinpointing her need for reasonable space and freedom.

She'd telephoned the Sockwith Insurance Bureau and was told that Lenny had rung in sick. She decided to go to his home, suspecting the illness may been catalysed by his misunderstanding surrounding the status of her relationship with Ralph.

She walked up Cobblestone Street, excited by her headline news.

The sun glared down on the bright white pavilion in the park. A few children wildly kicked a football around.

She reached the red door of number four, Leonard's car parked outside as normal. She pressed the bell button. A strained squeal responded inside, the buzzer's batteries on the point of expiry. There was no answer. She peered in the front window. There was no movement. She took a few steps backwards, looking up at his bedroom window. The curtains were closed. She did not want to postpone her news. She pressed the door buzzer once more, the squeal straining itself into ultimate silence. It sounded like a seagull with laryngitis, she thought.

She looked around the front concrete yard and picked up a few pebbles, carefully throwing them at his bedroom window. They tapped gently on the glass, as if given strict instructions not to cause any breakage.

Still no answer. She stood for a while. Then she walked into the park, past the boisterous children, stopping at the fence lining Lenny's back garden. She knew there was no access into the houses from the back. She sort of hoped that either a hole might have appeared in the fence, or at the least, she might see some movement through the back upstairs window.

Finally she gave up. She walked back down Cobblestone Street, into the village centre, peeped in each of the three pubs and then went on to the tea shop to relinquish Ginny for the afternoon.

"Hi, Ginny."

"Hi there, how are you today?" responded Ginny. Her earrings today were even larger, longer and more ridiculous than normal, like two crystal chandeliers, their transparent tips stroking her shoulders.

"Oh, I'm fine." She put on her pink chequered apron,

wrapping it twice round her small waist and tying it in a large bow. "I've been trying to get hold of Lenny. Apparently he's off work sick. I've tried to get him at home but he won't come to the door. I suppose he must be fast asleep."

"What's the urgency?"

"Well, you know I met Ralph yesterday and we went for a meal at the Blunt Raisin?" Chris explained, Ginny nodding. "Well, we discussed our relationship and we agreed it was best all round if we called it a day."

"Really?" responded Ginny, surprised. "I saw Lenny in the square yesterday afternoon and he was definitely under the impression you were pretty much an item."

"I know, Gin. He got it all wrong. Anyway, I've decided I want to get back with Len, if he'll have me."

"Of course he'll have you!" Ginny cried. She beamed from chandelier to chandelier, almost illuminating them. "He'll be over the moon! You must tell him! Have you tried telephoning him at home?"

"Err - no I haven't," Chris admitted.

"Well do it! Ring him now! He's bound to hear the phone ring!" Virginia urged, pushing the café phone at her as she spoke.

Chris lifted the receiver and excitedly tapped the buttons. She paced up and down behind the counter, phone in one hand, earpiece held to her ear with the other. "Come on, Len, come on!" she breathed. The telephone rang and rang and rang. Still no answer. "I don't understand it!" she said "Surely he hasn't unplugged it?"

"Try a bit later."

"Yes, I will. I've got to put him out of his misery. I don't want to get on that minibus tomorrow with him not knowing. And I won't be able to explain it to him in front of everyone else, will I?"

"Just try later," she encouraged. "It'll be all right, I'm sure."

Virginia untied her apron and went out the back. "Right I'm going out for a few hours, Chris. I'll be back by four, okay?" She emerged again, her hair released from the myriad of clips and pins, now draping down her back, the flow diverted at the sides by those immense jingling chandeliers.

At exactly five o'clock Ralph arrived back at the bus station, finalising his work for the day. He prided himself on his punctuality. He parked the bus in its allocated place, removed the cash bag and ticket machine, checked the bus to ensure everyone had alighted and leapt through the hissing doors.

Across the yard stood the tall, bearded, suited figure of Arbuthnot Clamp.

Parmesan tutted. His footsteps echoed as he approached Clamp. "Just be polite. See what we wants," he repeated under his breath.

"You wanted to see me, sir," he began, firmly but courteously.

"Yes. Just a brief chat. Come to my office, will you?" the Chief replied sternly.

Clamp swung open the door leaving it to rebound as Ralph followed. They clattered up the wooden stairs, Ralph behind him, studying the man's perfectly pressed trouser legs, black socks and black patent shoes. At the top of the staircase Clamp again swung open the door, this time touching it to prevent it assaulting his employee. They walked, one behind the other, down the long carpeted corridor to the end office, a brass sign heralding the Chief Executive's name and position. They entered, Clamp pointing to the chair designated for Parmesan. Ralph sat. Clamp walked round his huge desk and lowered himself into his large, black PVC recliner, air wheezing out as he sank.

"Right," began Clamp, hands grasped in front of his mouth, fingers pointing upwards. "I want to be straight with you, Ralph and I want you to reciprocate."

"He called me Ralph!" he reflected, concluding that he must be planning a soft approach. He decided to remain silent, awaiting further tactical revelations .

. "Let's put it to you this way, " Clamp continued, thumbing his ear in slight irritation. "You think you know something about my past that may be damaging. I don't know what that 'something' can be and therefore, unless you can enlighten me further, I'm going to take drastic action against you. Do you understand?" The Chief was now leaning forward with an authoritative, insistent tone.

Ralph continued to think, deciding to maintain his silence.

"Look, Parmesan..." Clamp was beginning to squirm, "When you mentioned Griswald's the other week, you caught me by surprise. I impulsively reacted by offering you some... err... 'sweeteners'... to avoid any future problems."

He looked up at Ralph again, tapping his fingers on his blotter. Still he was silent. Clamp writhed on his plastic chair and slapped the table in frustration. "The point is, Parmesan, having given it some thought, I can tell you nothing happened at Griswald's that incriminates me in any way. You've got nothing!"

The statement was entirely unconvincing. His voice was beginning to warble nervously.

After a pause, he angrily slammed the desk with both hands, pushed back his chair and paced over to Ralph. He stood right in front of him, bent down, his face close to Ralph's, his hands itching to grab the young man's neck.

Clamp gritted his teeth. "Right, Parmesan," he snarled. "You've had your chance..." He reached out with his right hand, grabbed Ralph's collar, twisting it, dribbling between his growling fangs and hissed: "You're bloody sacked!"

Ralph arose calmly, slowly, stood bolt upright and in turn reached for Clamp's tie. "Sacked, am I?" he challenged, squeezing the knot into a sausage shape. "I don't think so, Mister Clamp!" He pressed his nose closer to Clamp's. "I guessed you'd try to wriggle and squirm your way out of this. But it won't work."

He released the man from his grip and poked him in the chest. "As insurance against your pathetic denials and bluffs, I've already arranged to meet the press. If you really want reminding of your miserable past at Griswald's - as if you don't already know – you'll be able to read all about it, won't you?!"

"You're bluffing! I don't believe a word of it!" spat Clamp, trying to conceal his fear but his bearded bottom lip beginning to vibrate.

"Oh yes?" Parmesan continued "Bluffing, eh? If you don't believe me, just ring the Sockwith Weekly. I'm sure they would love to hear from you, eh?"

"Get out of my office!"

At that moment, the Accountant barged in. "Oh, sorry, sir!" he apologised, realising his intrusion was ill-timed, his face matching the crimson of his bow tie. He retreated, noticing Clamp's foaming mouth, closing the door quietly.

"Now, get out of my office, Parmesan!"

"Does that mean I'm sacked or not?" Ralph grinned, proceeding to the door.

"GET OUT!"

Ralph swung the door open and left, leaving it wide open. Then he poked his head round the door frame and added: "I've got the day off tomorrow, so you've got a day to consider your position. I'll be in on Wednesday as usual. Bye." He waved his hand with derision.

Clamp sunk back into his seat, rocking back and forth uneasily.

Seven o'clock approached. Christine was worried. She still hadn't managed to contact Leonard. She'd repeatedly telephoned his number that afternoon. She wrapped herself up warm in her coat and left the house to meet Ralph in the Grinning Plank as agreed. She decided to make a detour via Leonard's house once more. His car was still parked outside, his bedroom light glowed a soft orange through the curtains. She tried the doorbell. It no longer uttered any sound. She pulled at the letterbox and it snapped back noisily, echoing down the hall. The curtains were still open downstairs. She peered in but the room was dark.

She hastened to the pub, the bitter cold wind gaining

momentum, snow beginning to fall, her collar up and hands firmly in her fur-lined pockets.

Bob Rack was moving round the pub, issuing information to some of the passengers for the next day's journey, confirming arrival and departure times.

Christine walked up to Ralph.

"Hi, Ralph. Shall we sit down and talk then?" She motioned to a table that was distant from the other regulars.

"Yes, I s'pose so.. " Ralph replied, tiredly.

They walked over and sat. Parmesan was most uneasy being placed away from his stool. He looked around the walls of the pub, noticing things that he would never have seen from his normal site.

"How's your day been?" she asked, unbuttoning her coat.

"Oh, all right." He stopped looking around, sat back and looked at her.

"Actually, I had another row with Clamp. He was trying to call my bluff and sack me. But it didn't work," he continued smugly, his left leg perched horizontally over his right. "I'm too clever for him!"

"As long as you know what you're doing."

"Yep," he replied confidently. "Right then. I've been considering things since our lunch yesterday," he said with some thought, "and I'd like to know what you think of this... " He produced a folded piece of A4 paper from his coat pocket, flattened it out and twisted it round for her to read.

"Basically what I've done is two columns: one for you and one for me, listing what we should each have."

He sat back again: "What do you think?" He was well aware of Christine's meticulous attention to money and, in his opinion, had tried his hardest to be diplomatic over his distribution of goods and chattels.

She perused it carefully before reacting. The column headed "Ralph" contained just three lines, her's 9 items.

Her column listed: clothes, cosmetics, jewellery, portable TV, handbags, all food, wicker bedroom chair, fluffy rabbit and chicken, all single account funds and half of joint account funds.

His column listed: The house, everything else in the house and half of joint bank account.

She sat pensively for a while, weighing up whether this was reasonable. "Have you taken any money out today, Ralph?" she asked quietly.

"No."

"Are you aware of how much is in our joint account?"

"No."

"I'll tell you. The closing balance after cheques and the credit card I have to settle for our meal, will be £5,622.33p. You are asking for everything in the house, including things like the washing machine and fridge freezer that I bought, plus two thousand eight hundred pounds odd?"

"Yeah."

"Well, I don't know, Ralph."

"Put it this way: presumably you are going to move back in with 'Mister Real Ale Floppy-Hair Mantelpiece'?" he said astutely.

"Well ..." She'd been taken by surprise: had it been that obvious? "Yes, I think so," she admitted.

"Presumably, he's got all those things, you know, the washing machine and stuff, so you won't be losing out, will you? And as far as the money is concerned, I've got used to using some of your funds when I really needed to. I won't have that luxury any more and it's unlikely that my wages, even with the pay rise that Clamp's sort of offered, will stretch to paying everything... do you see my point?"

Christine was still staring at the paper, deep in thought. "What about the house?"

"Well, I've paid the mortgage since we bought it and I'm going to stay there. So, it's only fair it becomes completely mine."

"We'll have to change the deeds and stuff to remove my name."

"That's okay."

"Give me a few minutes to think about it, Ralph."

"Right. I'll be at the bar. Another drink?"

"Err .. No, thanks." Christine reached into her inside pocket and produced a pen and paper and commenced work on some financial calculations. It was clear that writing off a few thousand pounds would have no noticeable impact on her wealth; it was an entirely negligible sum, even adding to that the other capital assets she'd purchased, such as the brown and white goods to which Ralph had referred.

"Ralph," she called, signalling her readiness to proceed. He came over and sat.

"What do you reckon, then?" he asked.

"Okay, I'll accept. But we need to do some things together first."

"Such as?"

"We need to close the joint account, or at least put it into my name. Secondly we need to put the house and mortgage into your name. And I would be happier if we could sign something between us agreeing to the settlement of the house, items and money I'm giving you. And don't forget that we might be clobbered for wedding cancellations so we may have to settle some penalties there as well, which, I think we should both contribute to."

"Fine. So you want some sort of signed agreement?"

"Yes. Don't you think that's fair? I mean, it works both ways: it means I can't come screaming to you about wanting the house or the washing machine or whatever and you can't come to me demanding more money. Do you see what I mean?"

"Yes. I've got no objections. Shall we shake on it?" he concluded, extending his right hand towards her.

"One thing first, Ralph."

"What?"

"We need to get this sorted out soon. Can you get some time off?"

"How about Thursday? I'll take some time off and.we can go to the bank and stuff."

"All right. I'll ring everyone and fix up appointments for Thursday then."

"Thanks, Chris. You've been great considering. I don't really love you but I'll always have a soft spot for you. No doubt I'll probably get wound up when I see you and The Real Ale Man together. But, well... " he shrugged.

"You'll get over it. I'm really glad we've settled all this. Thank you." She squeezed his hand and then ruffled his clump of hair amicably, saying "You're not a bad old sod really..."

"Right then... " Ralph clapped and rubbed his hands together and stood up. "I'll get back to my stool then."

"See you in the morning for Calais if I don't see you back at home tonight. I'll wake you up about 5:30."

chapter seven
pierre and passports

Larynx was unusually busy for 6:00am. People were gathering outside the General Store, quietly talking, huddled in their warm coats.

The minibus approached, made a three-point turn in front of the church and pulled up. The doors clunked open, two yellow lights came on and the passengers boarded. Ralph was first, heading for the long back seat. He slumped, shivering by the window. Christine sat next to him.

"Can we sit here?" questioned Reg, his round head half concealed in a large bobble hat.

"Yes, of course," Chris replied. Reg flopped into the corner opposite Ralph. Bob squeezed in between them.

"No Lenny, then?" enquired Chris quietly and tactfully, not wishing Ralph to overhear, regardless of their arrangements.

"No. He rang me late last night," replied Bob, the trip organiser. "He's got a nasty tummy bug and said it would be most unlikely. He was laid up in bed all of yesterday," he grinned, correcting himself, "that's when he wasn't on the loo!"

"But I kept ringing him," replied Chris, concerned.

"I know, I told him that you were trying to get hold of him. He said he'd been so sick that he'd unplugged the phone. He didn't want to have to get out of bed more than he had to!"

"Did you tell him why I wanted to talk to him?"

"No. We promised we'd leave that to you."

Reg was leaning forward, "The sooner he knows, the better. It would probably cure his bowels instantly!" he joked.

"Can you stick the heater on, driver?" yelled Ralph, trembling dramatically.

The other passengers were seated. A head of thick, permed hair moved on the headrest directly in front of Parmesan.

"Oh, God, it's that Frog," muttered Ralph to Christine, half wanting Pierre to hear.

"Leave it, Ralph," retorted Chris. "We don't want any trouble today. Just ignore him and he'll ignore you."

"Hmmph"

The bus moved off.

"This isn't a bus," Parmesan scorned to Chris, "this is a dustbin on wheels. You know I'm going to be driving one of the new superbuses soon? It's going to be great. Apparently they've got piped music and messages that flash up for the passengers, telling them which stop is next and stuff."

"You're quite excited aren't you?" Chris smiled.

"Oh yes! I'll be one of the first drivers in the country to experience the new beast!" he beamed proudly. "They'll even have air conditioning, not like this heap!"

Bob from the Minibus Company leaned forward, challenging Ralph: "This *is* a bus, Ralph. It's a Bedford CF340 Midibus: it may not be a whizz-bang double decker outfit, but it's still a bus!"

"Shut your gob! Do you know what the brake horsepower of my bus is?" scoffed Ralph, his knowledge on this subject detailed in the extreme. "My bus is 200bhp at just 2,200 rpm. What's the power of this junk-heap?"

"Don't know, Ralph, and I don't care to be honest," retorted Reg turning away out of disinterest.

"Well I'll tell you: it's a pathetic eighty! *Eighty!* Ha! A Robin Reliant could do better! *My* bus has got 75 seats. This has a measley seventeen *And* my bus has got heating!" He leant forward, hands on Pierre's headrest and shouted again: "Has this crapheap got a heater, driver?!"

The permed head turned round. "Do you mind not screaming in my ear?! Just shut it!"

"Shut yours, Frog," Ralph snapped back. Chris grabbed his arm and frowned sternly at him in remonstration. "He's going to get on my wick all day", he huffed, pointing to the perm. "I see you've got your beloved wife with you, Pants." he called, intimidatingly .

Pierre kept quiet, staring out the window into the black.

Pandora was squeezing his hand comfortingly. She was a petite woman, with short black hair, thick eyebrows, small eyes and large red lips that seemed to engulf the lower half of her face.

"They're like Laurel and Hardy, those two," continued Ralph, to no-one in particular, grinning. He watched Pierre's expression in the window's reflection. "I wonder if he knows who Laurel and Hardy are, being French," he tormented, knowing that, if Pierre had any sense he'd remain quiet and take all this abuse, the consequences of any retribution reaping untold damage on the Frenchman's marriage.

Pandora moved closer to Pierre, cuddling his arm and whispering warmth into his ear. Reg, noticing the adjacent volatility, piped up: "What are you all going to buy in Calais, then?"

Ralph was first to reply, loudly narrating to the bus full of passengers: "I'm going to buy loads and loads of lager. I'm going to get rat-faced on the ferry, even more rat-faced back at the pub tonight, then I'm going to go home, stick on the footie replay and stuff my gut full of baguettes and cheese! It's going to be bloody great!" He bashed his hands in excitement on the headrest, the permed head lunging forward. "I'm going to get *shit-faced!*"

"Well, beat that, Bob!" said Reg.

"Oh, I'll get some bottled beer, Trapiste, if they've got it and I'll get some fags for Lenny, seeing he couldn't make it."

"How about you, Chris?"

"Oh, just some wine, I think," she said quietly, watching Ralph drumming Pierre's chair. "Pack it in, Ralph, for God's sake. Otherwise I'm going to sit somewhere else."

He sat back for a minute. "What are you going to get, then, Reg? I don't suppose you can get real ale over there. A wasted trip if you ask me!" enquired Ralph, sarcastically .

"Well, I just want to go round the town and see what they've got, really," he said humbly.

"Sorry, Reg" Bob said, "but we're not going to have time for that. Because of the ferry times, we're only going to have enough time really to go to Mammouth. Mind you, you never know what you might find there... it's a huge hypermarket."

"Oh, can't I be dropped off in the town, Bob?" replied Reg, his round face showing disappointment.

"No, we're not allowed to do that, really. The Company has to keep to a tight schedule and strictly account for everyone. Unlike last year we've got a lot less time. The bus is literally going to drive off the ferry, drop us at the hypermarket for a few hours and then take us home. Sorry about that, mate."

"Doesn't matter, Bob. It's a day out, anyway."

The bus wended its way through the snowy Kent countryside for about two hours and arrived at the Dover port. It joined the long queue of other coaches, alongside a longer queue of cars, headlights, side lights and brakelights splashing light on the steamy bus windows. The bus crawled forward and the doors opened.

A uniformed man stepped on. He spoke to the driver and inspected some papers.

"Passports, please, ladies and gents," he called. The passengers reacted, reaching into bags and pockets. The man slowly moved down the bus, flipping each passport in turn open and shut. "Thank you, thank you," he repeated after glancing at each one.

Ralph opened his and Chris noticed the photograph. "My God! Is that you?" she laughed. She snatched it from his grip and showed it to Reg and Bob. They burst into laughter.

"Look at that ridiculous gawping smile!" roared Reg.

"Give it back, pillocks" grabbed Ralph, embarrassed. "Let's see yours then. I bet they're worse!"

Reg opened his, Bob leaning towards it: "Oh shit, Reg, you look like Mr Magoo... look, your eyes are all creased up and your mouths all curled up!"

He rocked with laughter.

"Who's Mr Magoo'?" asked Ralph, amused, leaning over and yanking it away. "Oh, I know, he's that short-sighted cartoon pratt!" He laughed threw it back at Reg.

"Passports, please," the man beckoned, his arm reaching towards Ralph. They all sniggered as the officer studied each picture. He smiled in reciprocation, thanked them and walked back to the driver. They spoke for a few more moments and the man left. The bus moved on, over a ramp, down a slope and onto the ferry, the indoor lights displaying the early morning faces. Coaches manoeuvred into their tight positions and engines ceased, one-by-one.

The passengers made their way up the ferry stairs to the warm corridors. Ralph headed straight for the bar, the others, mainly in pairs, bustled around the ship, studying the various breakfast menus and duty free wares.

Reg and Bob sat in the lounge bar, each with a cappuccino and a newspaper.

Christine came over and sat with them. "I don't believe him," she said, referring to Ralph's behaviour once more.

"What's he up to now'?" inquired Reg, behind his Independent.

"He's already drinking and its only... " she studied her tiny watch. "It's only quarter-to-nine. It's obscene. And he keeps digging at Pierre."

"Oh, just keep away from him," Reg replied dismissively.

"Yes," agreed Bob, "you're not responsible for him now, Chris. Just let him do what he wants. You enjoy yourself," he said encouragingly. "Let's go for a walk."

"Okay," she smiled. "Coming, Reg?"

"No, I'll stay here and keep our seats," he muttered, engrossed in an article on micro-breweries.

Bob and Chris strolled around the ferry. They stood outside in the cold, the freezing breeze chilling their faces. They watched the boat skillfully negotiating a reverse between concrete quays. The sun was beginning to glow, the sea reflecting a fiery glow. They went back into the warm and into the duty free shop. "Benson and Hedges, isn't it?" checked Bob.

"Yes", Chris replied. "Those ones." She pointed to a stack of gold boxes with the familiar logo that always reminded her of

The Cheese Murder

Leonard. He's smoked them as long as she could remember. "I miss him. I'd have loved to have been with him today," she said, picking up a pack of two hundred. "I'll get him these," she said.

"Well, I'll get him some too. I know they're unhealthy but Len will appreciate them anyway," he said affectionately.

They continued to walk round the shop, the duty free wines and spirits rattling, clanging and clinking in their racks.

The bus eventually drove off the ferry into the Calais sunshine and followed the procession of British coaches all seemingly heading to one of the two hypermarkets.

"What a dump!" cried Parmesan, taunting Pierre. He watched out of the window as the bus followed the coastal route. Tall tower blocks sprung out of the scruffy landscape, each painted a garish pink, blue or yellow. "Look! They're building even more of those gruesome flats over there!" he pointed. Building sites of half-finished structures dotted expanses of wasteland along the coastline. Ralph started trumpeting *Rule Britannia* and drumming the headrest once more. The bus continued through a few more estates, the buildings gradually shrinking in height.

"There it is!" exclaimed Ralph, rubbing his hands with relish.

"What?" questioned Reg.

"The booze market, of course!" Ralph was pointing at it as it approached, identifying the large red elephant logo. He was up and out of his seat before the bus had even reached the car park.

The driver pulled up, turned off the engine and stood up. Ralph was already at the front, agitating.

"Hold on a moment," instructed the driver, restraining Parmesan. "Now listen, please everyone," he called. "The time now is 10:45 British time, 11:45 French time. I would advise you all to keep your watches at British time so that we're all in agreement. So, it's a quarter-to-eleven, British time. You will have three hours here at Mammouth. Okay? Besides the main hypermarket, there's a café, restaurant and some smaller shops, so you can get your lunch here as well. You must all be seated back on this bus by 1:45. No later. We have to be back at the ferry and boarded by two-thirty, so you must be punctual."

Ralph was still bobbing up and down. He pushed past the driver impatiently, pulled open the doors and ran towards the entrance, gathering a massive trolley en route, slotting in a ten franc piece, provided by Bob to all the passengers in advance.

Everyone else still waited on the bus. "Are there any questions before you leave?" the driver continued, trying to ignore Ralph's rudeness. "Right. A quarter-to-two back here then," he repeated sternly.

The crowd hustled towards the shop, collecting trolleys and wheeling them in.

chapter eight
punch and tea

Pierre and Pandora LePants stood studying the long row of shelves displaying the hundreds of different wines. She picked up bottles. He took them, shook his head and put them back.

"Trust me, I know French wines!" he kept saying, selecting his own and depositing them carefully into the trolley. She stood there with a calculator adding up as he announced their respective prices in francs and cents.

Ralph Parmesan barged past them, dragging his trolley behind him. "Oy! Can't you see I want to get past, Frog Breath?!" he rapped. A trolley wheel rammed onto Pierre's shoe.

"You could try saying 'excuse me'" said Pandora, frowning up at Ralph.

"Just move!" he retorted, heaving at his trolley. The wheel clattered over Pierre's foot, scraping against his ankle.

"Ow!" shrieked Pierre, pulling his leg away. This was the last straw. He swung his arm, fist clenched, landing a punch on Parmesan's right cheek. Parmesan reeled backwards, falling into a group of other Britons, knocking three of them to the floor like skittles.

Ralph scrambled up, seething with rage and lunged at Pierre. Pierre grabbed Ralph's trolley full of lager cases and pushed it into his pelvis. Ralph rebounded, collapsing backwards once more.

A French security man appeared uttering a string of foreign abuse. Pierre said a few French words to the man who immediately bent down, grabbed Ralph's hands and dragged him away. Ralph was yelling "I'll tell your wife! I'm going to do it, bastard!"

Pierre wrapped his arm round Pandora and gestured back towards the wines. "What does he mean? What's he talking about?" squeaked the little woman.

"Nothing. He's trouble. Take no notice," Pierre replied,

coolly, inspecting another bottle.

Parmesan was escorted to an office in the main parade. A clean, smart man in uniform sat behind a desk, smoking a Gauloise. Ralph coughed, repelled by the pungent smoke.

"Now listen to me," said the man behind the desk in good English. "You British are very welcome in Mammouth: you spend a lot of money here and we're glad to take it. But we do not like your... how you say?... thuggery. If you wish to fight this other man, do it in your own country. You can beat up as many people there as you like, I don't mind. But not here. Comprehend, Monsieur?

"Yes. Sorry," replied Ralph quite sincerely. He was glad to have faced no more than a ticking off. He had feared expulsion, without the alcohol and food he'd planned for so long.

"Right. Go! Get back to spending your money on us and no more trouble!"

Parmesan left the office, his cheek hard, bruised, swollen. He returned to his trolley, laden with the six cases of lager and pushed it towards the delicatessen counters.

He joined the queue for cheeses. The smell was quite incredible; the most pungent cheeses mixed with the spicy odours from a wide display of cured meats, sauces and fruits. His turn arrived. The woman behind the counter nodded at him and he pointed to three cheeses. He knew no French of any use. He leant on the top of the long, perspex frontage that curved over the fresh food. The woman glared at him as the perspex began to sag. She ranted something unpleasant and gestured.

"Oh... " he muttered, standing upright, turning red from her obvious scolding. He mumbled as he continued to point and use his hands to describe the sizes he wanted cut from the large blocks. The woman silently cut each one, wrapped them and fixed a printed sticker. Ralph took them, nodded and said "Bonjour" in a polite effort to thank her. The woman grimaced. Ralph advanced the trolley to the bakery and selected three baguettes from a deep wooden unit. He stood for a minute, his nose .pressed on one, sniffing with pleasure. A man at the bakery looked at him. Ralph stuck his thumb up in approval and balanced the bread across the boxes of lager bottles.

"Hi, Ralph." It was Chris. "Have you got everything?" she asked looking casually into his trolley.

"Yeah. Six crates of Pils, some cheese and bread. That's all I need."

"Well, I've got some wine," she said. "That's enough for me."

They moved off down the aisle towards the checkout.

"Oh, hang on, Ralph," she said, noticing something on one of the shelves. She picked it up. It was a small teapot, designed for the single drinker. She felt it a shame that Leonard had relinquished tea leaves for a teabag in a mug because his teapot was too large and impractical. "He can use this when I'm out," she thought.

"What's that?" asked Ralph,

"It's a teapot, of course. I just like it." she said, holding it up proudly and affectionately - a sort of symbolic declaration, she thought, of the reunification of her and Len. The teapot was royal blue with brilliant yellow spots, the main body perfectly round, the lid nestling tightly in the top orifice.

"Yes, I like it" she repeated with satisfaction. Now I need some tea..."

Ralph followed slowly behind, disinterested, mimicking a million British husbands and boyfriends reluctantly accompanying their female partners on the weekly supermarket jaunt. He looked wholly vacant and useless. She picked up two tins of tea, both seeming unusual, and smiling, placed them alongside her other items.

They paid at the checkout and wheeled the loaded carts to the café for lunch. Most of the other passengers were already there, eating a variety of baguettes and pastries.

Pierre looked over his shoulder and noticed Ralph. They sat, trying to out-stare each other for a good three minutes. Ralph then screeched "I'm going to tell her! When you're not around I'm going to tell her!!"

The minibus drew up outside St Barnaby's Church as the clock struck 6:30pm. The journey had been long and tiresome. The majority of the passengers were relieved to get away from the claustrophobic and hostile atmosphere caused by Ralph, endured for the entire return trip.

"Get this stuff home for me," he ordered Chris, pointing to the pile of cases which had been pushed under the rear seats of the bus. "I can't wait to get to the pub."

"Here, we'll help," Reg and Bob offered. The threesome moved the boxes of drinks, food and other purchases off the bus. "You stay here with our beer, Chris, and we'll carry your stuff to your house," Bob said kindly. "We'll dump it by your front door, okay?"

The pair lifted the heavy cases, the carrier bag of bread and cheese, the bag containing Christine's wines, teapot and tins of tea and the 200 cigarettes bought for Leonard, and struggled with them to Christine's door, placing them on the step. They ran back to her.

"Thanks, chaps. You're very kind. I'd like to join you for a drink but I've got to meet Ginny. We're going out for the night See you tomorrow. Bye."

chapter nine
the end of the cheese

Ralph stumbled home, full to the brim with lager. He was managing to maintain reasonable control of his faculties, regardless of the volume he'd imbibed and was looking forward to flopping in front of the football match re-run on the Sports channel, accompanied by three baguettes and three french cheeses, purchased specifically for this special occasion. He desperately needed some substance to soak up the bucketful of gaseous liquid in his stomach.

He opened the front door, removed his black coat and dropped it on the hall floor. He went into the living room, the fire nicely glowing. Christine must have lit it before going out for the night, he thought smiling, reflecting on her thoughtfulness.

He switched on the television and hunted round the room, half in darkness, for the remote control. He slid his hands along the back of the sofa and, sure enough, there it was. He pointed it and pressed number 6. The room filled with an emerald green luminosity, sounds of football crowds and commentary. He turned the volume up loud to really soak up the atmosphere.

He moved into the kitchen, bent down towards the carrier bag that Christine had left propped up by the washing machine and withdrew one of the 12-inch baguettes. He put it to his nose and sniffed until his lungs were full. He opened the fridge and gathered together his three cheeses, reaching for a dinner plate with the other hand.

He moved back into the lounge, dragged a small coffee table over to the sofa using his foot, putting down the plate, the cheeses and the stick. "Knife... knife," he muttered and dashed back into the kitchen, returning with a cheese knife.

"Right," he said, positioning himself nearly prostrate on the sofa, the table by his head. He arranged a few cushions under his head and lay for a while engrossed in the premiership match.

"Come on, come on... cross it now! Now!" he urged the players, repeatedly grunting in disappointment at their inept performance.

He reached for the bread, unwrapped it from its crispy, transparent packaging and pulled a piece off, crumbs and pieces of crust dropping onto the table. He placed the torn-off chunk onto the plate and lifted up the three cheeses, close to his face, to read the labels the hypermarket had printed. He replaced two on the table and unwrapped the chosen one. Putting it on the plate, he lifted the knife and depressed it into the blue-veined texture, releasing a large, rectangular, creamy lump. He gently sliced off the rind and pressed the blue cheese firmly into the broken end of the bread.

Staring at the television he entered the bread and cheese into his wide open mouth, tearing off a huge piece and proceeding to chew. "Come on, come on," he mumbled while chewing, addressing the forwards with every run they made into the last third of the field. He continued to consume the bread and cheese for five more minutes and then lay back down for a rest, chewing and extracting smaller pieces nestling in the crevices of his mouth. He yawned and slowly drifted off to sleep, the football still in its first half.

About half an hour passed with Ralph fast asleep on the sofa, bread and cheese by his side.

A key rattled in the back door and a cold draft gusted momentarily through the house. A silhouetted figure entered. It wore large Wellington boots and a boilersuit and carried various items in both gloved hands. It walked quietly up to the sleeping Parmesan's head which was resting nearest to the kitchen door. The figure cautiously peered over him to ensure he was in deep sleep. Ralph was snoring heavily, mouth wide open.

The figure bent down, laying out various things on the floor. It unfolded a large black sheet: a dustbin liner which had been cut open to double its size, a hole incised in the middle, slightly larger than the diameter of Parmesan's head.

The silhouette gently and slowly placed it over the sleeping man, draping one end over the end of the sofa, the other end over Ralph's neck and chest, his head poking through the circular hole. Parmesan snorted, flinched and continued his deep sleep. The vast amount of alcohol consumed that day had, by now, rendered him close to unconsciousness.

The figure bent down again and, from a bag, selected a jagged length of french bread and topped it with a huge chunk of orange, rubbery cheese, both brought as part of the cunning plan. This had been prepared in advance to economise on time in finding Ralph's own bread and cheese – and, crucially, the cheese had been specially selected for its adhesive, non-porous properties. The broken stick was about eight inches long and just under two inches in diameter. The cheese was gently held on whilst the figure directed the bread towards Parmesan's open, snoring mouth.

Then, in one almighty moment, the figure thrust the stick, cheese first, plunging it into Parmesan's mouth, pushing it and pushing it until the cheese could travel no further, causing a seal around the man's throat and windpipe. Ralph's lips stretched and stretched as the bread was pushed in, wrapping tightly and thinly round the baguette's circumference. The gloved figure stood over Ralph's head, gripping the pointed end of the depressed bread in position.

Parmesan snorted through his nose, attempting to inhale air. But the cheese had denied oxygen any access to his gullet and lungs. He began to writhe, his hands rising to seek out the offender. His sore, red eyes were open, staring wildly upwards, seeing nothing but a pair of arms reaching down towards his mouth. Parmesan's reflexes instructed him to bite the bread, to break it in his mouth and relieve the pressure on his elasticated lips. He started to gnaw viciously, his teeth sinking violently into the bread, his head shaking from side to side, like a lion dismembering its prey. The figure above him continued to press firmly on the bread, pushing and squashing it, flakes of crust dropping in the struggle.

Ralph started to weaken, his writhing arms and legs finally submitting, his eyes rolling, his nose pumping out small globules of loose cheese and saliva that had been sucked up from his throat. He closed his eyes, groaned internally for a lengthy ten seconds and then flopped like a discarded glove puppet.

His teeth were still heavily pressed into the bread - with such force that blood had started to seep from his gums. The corners of his lips had begun to crack from the tension, like a thick rubber band stretched to splitting point.

The figure stood over him for a minute, motionless, ensuring all life had expired.

It then moved round the table, knelt and studied Parmesan's face. Bubbles of saliva mixed with breadcrumbs and blood were shining and dribbling around his mouth, each reflecting the second half of the match like minute television screens. The force of his gnawing jaw had accentuated a large hard lump of bone and muscle which ran under his flesh from beneath his chin into his neck, met by a profusion of protruding veins and muscles. His Adam's Apple appeared to be on the point of popping out, restrained only by a thin membrane of skin.

The killer lifted the left over chunk of bread belonging to Ralph from the table and placed it on the bin liner on the dead man's chest, substituting the remainder of the killer's baguette, so that the texture and tear would match the piece rammed into his mouth. The rest of the orange rubbery cheese which had hermetically sealed Ralph's windpipe was placed onto the plate alongside the blue cheese and rind, again breaking a few pieces off and dropping them around the plate and table. The killer picked up the cheese knife by the blade's hook, turned it perpendicular to the rubbery cheese and pressed the top of the blade until it was virtually concealed in the cheese. This manoeuvre avoided smudging Ralph's fingerprints on the handle.

The killer then reached out to Ralph's left hand, draped by the side of the sofa, lifting it and sniffing his fingers. As guessed, he would have held the cheese with his left hand whilst cutting with his right. Ralph's hand was then directed to the rubbery cheese, his fingers pressed into it, then dropped back, his arm flopping naturally back against his side.

The killer placed the original broken bread and its wrapper into a carrier bag, substituting the new wrapper, accompanied by the rubbery cheese packaging. One of the other unopened cheeses bought by Ralph earlier that day was then selected by the figure and placed in the bag for disposal.

It would now appear, the killer hoped, that Ralph had got atrociously drunk, opened and began two of his three cheeses, fallen into a senseless stupour halfway through eating and suffocated on the food. The evidence would show the three cheeses, two with opened packaging the third still wrapped, part of a baguette, the remainder of which was stuffed in his mouth, the other two loaves still in the carrier bag in the kitchen - all closely conforming to Ralph's procurements in France, should any witnesses be approached for confirmation.

The figure stood over Ralph's body and gently rolled up the bin-liner. The sheet was carefully pulled away from the dead man's head, avoiding the french stick protruding from his swollen mouth. Having fully removed the sheet, the killer scrunched it up tight, retaining all the crumbs, and placed it in the carrier bag. The sheet had served the useful purposes of protecting the killer from any contact with the body or the immediate vicinity, in case of any later inspection by forensics.

The murderer then walked to the back door, pulled the key from a breast pocket and locked it. The calm figure switched on the kitchen light and reached into the Mammouth bag containing the two unopened loaves and rummaged, intending to find the receipt, listing the details of the original bread and cheese. It wasn't there.

The light was extinguished and the killer moved around the lounge, looking for Ralph's jacket, and then into the hall. Picking up the jacket, it removed one glove and delved into the pockets, vision strained in the near-darkness, checking various pieces of paper. Still no receipt. The papers were replaced and the coat thrown back onto the floor.

The figure returned to Ralph. The killer knelt by Ralph's groin and slid the ungloved hand into one of Ralph's front pockets. A warm, damp handkerchief greeted the interrogating fingers. The hand went to the other front pocket, groping amongst loose change and a folded piece of paper. The paper was extracted and held to the light from the television. It was a ten pound note. Carefully folded back up, it was pushed back into the pocket. The hand squirmed into Parmesan's back left pocket, squeezed between heavy buttock and cushion. It was empty. The final pocket was on the far side, nearest the back of the settee. The figure leant over him and heaved at his right buttock, levering Ralph's solid, weighty pelvis towards him. Ralph's stomach emitted slopping sounds in response to the movement. The killer's naked hand quickly slipped into this final pocket and pulled out several small ticket-shaped pieces.

Standing up and turning towards the light from the television, Ralph's body settling back into position, the silhouette inspected them. One was indeed the receipt! It clearly listed, in French, the bread, the three cheeses and six crates of lager. The other piece of paper was a torn-off strip from a newspaper, showing a newsroom telephone number. Both bits were placed deep in the carrier bag with the other items for removal and disposal.

A roar went up - at last someone had scored! The figure stood calmly watching the eight replays of the goal, turned the television off with gloved hand, scanned the scene of death, picked up the carrier bag of evidence, put on the other glove and left by the front door, shutting it firmly but quietly.

chapter ten
shock and suspicion

The snow had continued to fall throughout the night. A layer of ice covered the village roads. The Christmas lights glowed in the misty morning air. Reg was outside the store scraping and shovelling with a garden spade.

"Morning!" he called, noticing Christine crossing the road opposite with her overnight bag. "Have a good night?"

"Yes, it was good fun," she said approaching him. Her nose was red from cold, her cheeks pink. "God, it's freezing today."

"Yeah."

"See you later," she said and crunched along the pavement, crossing the road to her front gate. She pushed it hard, dislodging the snow that had built up against it. She reached into her pocket and took out her key. It was past ten o'clock. She expected to be alone in the house.

She put down her bag and removed her gloves and coat, shutting the door. Ralph's jacket was on the floor. She picked it up, curious. Perhaps, she thought, he drank too much and has overslept?

"Ralph?" she called, hanging his and her coats in the cupboard under the stairs.

"Ralph?" she called again, climbing the stairs to check the bedroom. There was no sign of him. The bed hadn't even been slept in. She went downstairs, expecting to find him asleep on the floor or the settee.

She entered the lounge and saw him "Ah, there you are..." she began, seeing him flat out. Then she noticed his face.

She emitted a horrifying scream: a scream that caused virtually every object in the house to tremble close to shattering; a scream that seemed to resound for miles. She stood there, clutching the sides of her head, screaming and screaming, staring at the gruesome scene. The more she stared, the more she screamed.

In the bright light of day, the picture was horrible. Ralph's face was pale, a dove-greyish pale. His eyelids were a blueish pale. His stretched lips were a pinkish pale. The length of baguette still protruded from his mouth, like a stake that had been hammered in. A trickle of blood had turned purple down his chin. Yellow flecks of saliva and cheese had dried around his nose and mouth like ripe spots full of pus.

An awful smell filled the room, quite unidentifiable: was it the cheese that had been left out all night or was it Ralph? Or both?

The screams stopped. Christine jolted as if she'd been slapped round the face and she ran into the road. A few people were standing nearby having heard the screams, unsure of their place of origin.

She ran past them, trudging through the snow, into the shop. The bell clanged with great urgency. "Reg..." she whimpered, unable to say more. He looked up from behind the post office grill. Her expression was frightening. He disappeared, locking the post office door and appeared in the shop.

"What the hell is it?"

She stood there, shaking wildly.

"Show me!" he demanded, grabbing her arm. They ran together to her house.

She stood in the hall and pointed into the lounge. Reg poked his head round the corner.

"Oh my God," he whispered, hardly believing the sight that beheld him. He slowly approached the body. "Oh my God. He's dead... from his own baguette. Bloody hell. The police, Chris... have you rung the police?"

"Err, no... no..."

"I'll do it. Where's your phone?"

She stood by the front window, frozen to the spot, pointing to the phone, still shaking.

"Police, please... thanks... " he said. He kept looking at Ralph. "He must have been well gone to have died like that," he said, shaking his head. "Oh, police? Yes. I'm at err... Chris, what number house is this?"

"Ten"

"Number ten, Church Lane, Larynx. A man's dead... Yes... err... Reg Book... Yes... Phone number? Err.. 451665... okay, see you in a minute."

He walked up to Christine and cuddled her. Her arms were fixed firmly by her sides, stiff from shock.

"Come on, Chris." He shook her gently. "Go into the kitchen and make some coffee," he said slowly and clearly. She responded, still in a trance, sidling past the corpse and into the kitchen.

A few minutes passed without a sound. Reg called to her: "Chris? Have you got the kettle on, love?" There was silence.

He went in there. She stood, staring out the window, still stiff. He held her hand.

"Come on, put the kettle on, Chris. If you occupy yourself, you won't feel so bad..." He guided her, holding her waist, towards the kettle. He unplugged it and handed it to her. "Take it, Chris, take the kettle." She was useless. Reg gave up and did it himself.

They stood in the kitchen, Reg with his arm around her, both staring out of the icy window.

The police arrived, letting themselves in.

"Hello?" one of them called. It was Vivian Fledgling, the pretty young Constable who had handled Arbuthnot Clamp so well after the Archie Pond death.

Reg walked though the house to meet them. "Hello, it was me that rang you... err... It's him," he said, pointing around the lounge door to the body.

The two officers walked into the lounge. "Is this your house, sir?" asked Fledgling, quietly.

"Oh, no, I was called here after he was found . It's Chris's house."

"Chris?"

"Yes. She's in the kitchen. Very shocked."

Fledgling went through to the kitchen. "Hello, Chris. I'm Constable Vivian Fledgling. Are you all right?"

"Mmm," responded Christine.

"Can you tell me what happened, love?" she asked softly.

"I just came in and there he was." she said flatly, still staring out the window.

"When did you come in, Chris?"

"About ten this morning."

"Is he your boyfriend or husband or...?"

"My ex-boyfriend."

"I see," Fledgling commented, puzzled. "Can you tell me exactly what happened, please?"

"Do you want a cuppa?" asked Chris, turning, her consciousness somewhat reinstated.

"Yes, please. Can you do one for Colin as well, please?"
"Who?"

"Oh, my colleague in there, he's another Constable: Constable Colin Teeth."

"Oh. Okay." She lifted the lid from the steaming kettle and poured a jet of water into it from the sink tap, plugged it in and clicked it on.

"What happened was this," she began, staring out the window once more. "I came to the door - I'd stayed over at a friend's for the night - it was about ten o'clock. I opened the door and came in. Ralph's coat was lying on the hall floor. I didn't expect him to be here. I thought he'd be at work. I thought perhaps he'd overslept because he had a real skinful yesterday. I hung up his coat and my coat..."

"You hung his coat up?" interrupted Fledgling, scribbling madly.

"Yes. Then I went upstairs, calling him. He wasn't up there so I came down here." She paused and shuddered, re-living the nightmare. "I just saw him there - as he is now. I screamed. I ran out and fetched Reg. He works in the post office. We ran back and he rang you. That's it."

"So when did you last see Ralph, prior to today?"

"Last night. A whole lot of us had been to France on a day trip and we got back about half-six. Ralph went straight to the pub, already quite drunk. I came back here, got changed and went into Sockwith to meet my friend Ginny."

The kettle bubbled, the switch flicked to 'off' and PC Vivian handed Chris two mugs.

"So you say he was your ex-boyfriend, is that right?"

"Yes. We'd just split up - quite amicably - and I was about to move out. Strictly it's his house."

"Right, so you still live here but only temporarily?" the policewoman checked.

"Yes." Chris made two coffees to the Constable's instructions and Fledgling carried them both into the lounge. Three more men had arrived on the scene, two in plain clothes.

"Hello, Vivian," greeted one of them. It was DI Brian Fluids. "I knew this chap vaguely," he explained quietly to her, nodding towards the body. "You remember the Archie Pond incident?"

"Oh yes?" confirmed Fledgling.

"Well," continued Fluids, "this was the chap that accused Clamp of Pond's murder. Stan Stringent and I visited him here that same day... Is the girl in there?"

"Yes, in the kitchen."

Fluids went in to see Chris. "Hello, Miss Ribcage, this must be an awful shock. I'm so sorry."

"Yes," she replied.

"Was he drunk?"

"Yes. Very."

"Mmm." Fluids pondered and then elaborated: "At first sight it looks like a really tragic accident, what you might call misadventure. He must have fallen into a state of unconsciousness while eating and literally suffocated on his food. Odd, I know, but that's how it looks..."

"I can't believe it," Chris replied. "He's often collapsed from a drunken stupor but I can't believe that he could die whilst eating. He was really looking forward to his cheese and bread after the pub."

Stringent, the bungling uniformed cop, was leaning, listening at the kitchen doorway.

"Well, at least he died happy, then!" he commented, grinning. Fluids glared at him and gestured to him to go back into the lounge away from sensitivity.

"So," Fluids continued with more questioning, "this cheese and bread - he got it yesterday in France, did he?"

"Yes - the rest of his bread's down there in the bag and his beer's over there." The yellow cases were stacked up in a corner.

Fluids returned to the scene. The other plain clothes man, a forensics expert, was peering over the body humming. He gently levered the bread from side to side to try to get a view inside Ralph's elasticated mouth.

"Any joy, Halibut?" asked Fluids.

"Well, there doesn't seem to be anything suspicious but it's early days," the forensic man replied, pouring over the body. He straightened up, then leant over and reached for a camera. He hummed as he toured the scene, clicking and flashing, capturing Ralph's gruesome state and the neighbouring cheese on film in great detail.

"Get everything bagged up," Halibut directed, "The cheese, the knife, the bread, the plate and anything else you can find that may be useful. Let's get him carted off."

Christine had entered the room, watching with some horror. "Are you taking him away now?" she asked.

"Yep," said Stringent "We'll drag him down the lab, slice him up a bit and have a good look," he said bluntly. His lack of tact triggered Christine's sobbing once more.

"For God's sake, Stringent!" charged Fluids, "Have you no tact? Can't you see this girl's in an awful state? Just keep your trap shut, okay?"

"Sorry, sir... I thought I was..." began Stringent, fumbling with his hat.

"Just shut up and leave!" Fluids ordered, pushing him

towards the door.

The other officers were carefully collecting various items together and placing them in polythene bags.

"Would you like me to stay with you for a while, Chris?" asked Vivian. Chris nodded, sniffing and inspecting her handkerchief for a dry patch. Fledgling conjured up a bunch of tissues and thrust them at her.

Some time later the other officers quietly left and two men came in with a trolley to transport Ralph to the van. "Do you want to go out or into another room while they move Ralph?" asked Fledgling.

"No, I'm all right," Chris whimpered. "I can hardly see anything anyway," she said, trying to smile.

The two men moved the coffee table aside and pulled the trolley parallel with the sofa. One man stood at Ralph's head, the other at his feet. Quietly, one counted to three and they lifted him. Lying flat, one man unruffled a red sheet and gently draped it over Parmesan. Chris watched as the trolley was pushed out of the room: the sheet showing little shape except where it rose sharply over the protrusion of bread.

Leonard Mantlepiece came rushing into the house. "Chris!" he called, running up to her, prizing her away from the woman Constable. "Oh, Chris, my darling, I've just heard!" He cuddled her tightly, squeezing out a new wave of tears.

"Where've you been?" she sobbed. "I've been trying to reach you for days."

"I've been sick, Giblet. What happened? Reg told me he was dead from some bread or something... what was it: food poisoning?" he asked, muddled. He wiped her eyes with the wodge of tissues and stroked her hair. Vivian Fledgling put her hand on Leonard's and questioned him.

"Excuse me, dear, what's your name then?"

"Leonard. Leonard Mantlepiece. I'm a friend of Chris's.

What happened? Tell me."

"Well, we don't really know yet, Leonard. Do you mind if I ask you a few questions whilst you're here?"

"What now? It's not really the right time or place, with Chris in this state, is it?" he said firmly, continuing to caress her.

"Len, talk to her. Let's get this over with," encouraged Christine, her arms now around his neck.

" All right. Presumably you want to know where I was when this happened?"

"Yes. We think he died last night, probably around midnight. "

"Well, I was in bed. I've spent the last two days laid up with a tummy bug, you know, 'the runs'."

"Can anyone confirm that?"

"Err, no..." he said.

"Chris," Vivian continued, "We don't know whether this was accidental or not at the moment. If we assume it wasn't accidental, could you tell me of anyone who might have had good reason to... " Her normal soft, caring femininity was transforming to the harder side of her professionalism,

"What, kill him?" she responded, shocked at the suggestion.

"Yes."

"Well, I don't know. Err... " She had to think for a while. "He wasn't particularly popular, I s'pose, but I'm not sure about anyone wanting to do *this* to him!"

"Not popular? What do you mean?" she asked pursuing the matter further.

"Well, he did tend to cause trouble," she said, sounding ashamed at being associated with him.

"Trouble? With whom?" persisted Fledgling, her expression becoming more severe with each question.

"Well, he was being a right pain only yesterday. He had a fight and was making threats, but..." she considered Pierre as a potential killer for a moment and, dismissing him, continued, "No, Pierre wouldn't have done this."

"Pierre?" questioned the WPC.

"Pierre?" repeated Leonard looking shocked. "What happened, then?"

"Oh, it was nothing... just a niggly argument," she continued, further dismissing the incident as motive for murder.

"I need to know, Christine," insisted Vivian. "Pierre *who?* Where does he live? What happened?"

Christine relayed an account of the past few days' confrontations between the two hot-heads.

"I never knew about all this trouble!" interjected Lenny at various points. "This sounds serious," Lenny said forcefully. "And he was outrageously cruel and violent to you! You can't rule him out, Chris!"

Christine was dumbfounded at this real prospect.

"Anyone else, Chris?" questioned the officer, rapidly scribbling in her notebook.

"Me, I suppose," Mantlepiece volunteered. "I disliked the man intensely and I wanted Christine back: we used to be an item, you know," he said, clutching Chris's hand.

"Don't be daft, Len," dismissed Christine.

"Well," continued Leonard, waving his hands with certain submission, "if you think about it, I had a motive of sorts: not as serious as Pierre's but... "

"That's stupid, Leonard. You had no motive at all! You and I are back together anyway," she said, smiling affectionately.

"What? What are you talking about?"

"Oh, of course - you don't know, do you?" she exclaimed. "I never got round to telling you. Ralph and I split up at the weekend."

She swept back her hair, pouted sensuously, flung forward her arms and announced: "I've decided to come back to you!" Her entire disposition had transformed from utter grief to utter excitement.

Leonard was still, except for his mouth which silently opened and closed like a goldfish. He went a ghostly pale. And then he smiled a smile of the greatest magnitude. His eyes shone with a new-found light. His suppression of affection was over. With an unreserved passion, he thrust his entire body towards her. He pushed her against the wall, one arm snaked up her jumper routing for her breasts, the other madly fiddling with the button on her jeans. He licked and slobbered every patch of her face, like a salivating hound. His frantic body smothered the girl, enveloping her under a panting, writhing mass of lust and relief.

Fledgling cleared her throat loudly.

"Lenny, Lenny!" Chris yelped from somewhere beneath him. She pushed him away and reappeared, dishevelled and mis-shapen, her entire facial features coated in an amorous wetness.

"Sorry!" trembled Lenny, straightening his clothing. "I can hardly believe it!"

"You didn't know about this before now?" questioned the officer suspiciously.

"Well, no ... but... this is fantastic!" His passionate appetite was priming him to resume his primitive foreplay. It hurt him to resist.

"Mr Mantlepiece!" snapped the WPC, reinstating formality.

"Oh, come on, Constable, you're not serious? Me? Kill Ralph?" He stood there distressed at her implications and annoyed at her inhibitive presence.

"We can't rule anyone out. But, like you said, you did have a motive."

Lenny was side-tracked again. He stared boyishly at his lover, glazed and dazed. "Oh, Giblet," he sighed.

"Please, sir! Control yourself! This is a serious matter!" Fledgling scolded.

Chris put her arm around his waist. "I assure you, officer, Lenny couldn't kill a moth, let alone a monster like Ralph!". Fledgling ignored her and continued.

"How about yourself, Miss Ribcage? You were separating from the deceased you say?"

"Yes but we'd already sorted it all out. It was all totally amicable."

"Would you stand to gain anything with him out the way?"

"Please, officer," Leonard whined, "We want to be alone. I *need* to be alone with her. I can hardly control myself. Surely this can wait?" He began pecking and fumbling again.

"I'm sorry you two but I must have some answers. The sooner you co-operate, the sooner you can get on with 'it'. Now. Miss Ribcage, please answer me. What do you gain by Mr Parmesan's death?"

"Nothing that I *need!*" Chris exclaimed.

"But what will you get?" she persisted.

"The house. I'll inherit the house. It's still in joint names," she huffed. "But I don't *need* it. I've got nearly a quarter of a million pounds, Constable. So I don't need this... do you see?"

"It's in joint names, is it? You said earlier that it was his?" she said, industriously flicking back in her notes.

"Yes it is in joint names but we'd agreed he should have it. As I say, I've got more than enough money."

"Any life insurance policies?"

"Well, yes, but... "

"And now you're pairing up with Mr Mantlepiece!" her suspicions becoming overpoweringly offensive to the couple.

"Well, yes, but..."

"So, with the sale of this house, plus Ralph's life assurance, you'll inherit what? Another hundred thousand?"

"Well, more than that, but..."

"How much more than that, Miss Ribcage?"

"I don't know... a few hundred, I suppose. But..."

"Thank you. I think that's all for now," she interrupted, packing her book away. "I'll keep in touch." She moved towards the door, then stopped, adding: "Halibut, the forensic chap will be back in a minute. Please try not to touch anything. This may have been a tragic accident but there's a lot to do." She left sharply.

"My God! She suspects me!" Chris exclaimed.

"And me," said Len.

"She even thinks we might have done this together."

chapter eleven
the case of halibut

Lenny sat with Christine sprawled across him on the armchair. They were enthusing about their new life together, their elation occasionally interspersed with references to Ralph's demise. Although it was tragic, their excitement far outweighed the morning's shock.

There was a knock on the door.

Christine clambered off the chair and opened the front door, recognising the visitor as the forensic detective who had initially inspected the scene. He was a small stocky chap, virtually concealed within a shabby raincoat and deer stalker, his worn-out face lined with silvery bristles.

"Halibut," he greeted her. "I'm the forensic..."

"Come in, Mr Halibut," said Chris.

The small man wandered in and nodded at Leonard. "I need to check out various things, Miss Ribcage. If you wish to go out and let me get on, that's fine. You don't have to stay."

"I'd rather stay, if you don't mind."

"Fine," he said, removing his hat and looking for somewhere to place it which wouldn't impede his work. "I'll put my hat here," he said, placing it on the carpet in front of the blackened fireplace. "Right," he continued., "I'll just get on then."

"Would you like a cuppa?"

"No thanks. I'll just get on." He started traipsing up and down the lounge, carefully surveying everything in the room, digesting every detail. He monotonously hummed as he paced. Chris and Lenny sat back on the armchair and watched in silence.

"That table's been moved, yes?" Halibut asked, pointing at the coffee table.

"Your men moved it when they... when they took Ralph

away," explained Chris.

"Right," he answered, efficiently continuing his perusal of the room. He recommenced his humming, pacing into the kitchen. Chris and Lenny looked at each other, amused at the man's strange ways. The humming loudened and then stopped dead. The man muttered something.

"Pardon?" responded Chris, rising and looking into the kitchen. Halibut was on all fours, his head on the ground studying the crack under the back door. "Nothing, ignore me. I'll just get on." He hummed again then reappeared in the lounge. He was scratching his head. "Err, Miss Ribcage. Do you have a back doormat?"

"No."

"Right. I'll get on then." And he disappeared again.

"Can you pass me my bag, please," he called. Chris got up, looking around for it. "Where is it?" she called.

"Oh... I think I left it on the very bottom stair when I came in. Thanks."

She went into the hall and picked up an old tatty tan case with the initials HHH crookedly glued onto it. "Here," she said, walking into the kitchen.

"Err, careful where you tread. I think there's something here," he snapped. "Put it by the sink," he instructed, lying on his front on the floor. She looked down at him, amused at his small size and shape, sprawled on the lino like a little child playing with an imaginary toy. His thin grey hair encircled a large shiny baldness containing an array of dark freckles. "Have you got any wellies?" he asked, his lips virtually kissing the ground.

"No."

"What about your husband?"

"You mean Ralph?"

"Mmm," he said, getting up and brushing himself down. "Has he got any wellies?"

"No."

"Mmm. I thought not." He pensively stroked his chin, the spikes fizzing like an agitated nailbrush. "Who came in here yesterday?"

"No-one." she said, concerned at his implications of intrusion.

"Well you know that's not true!" he observed.

"What do you mean?" she asked, puzzled.

"Well, you did. And clearly your husband did!"

"Yes - *we* did. But no-one else," she admitted, confused.

"Mmm. Thought so. Right. I'll get on then." And he ushered her out of the way and knelt by the arm of the sofa where Ralph's head had laid. "Mmm. Touched anything here?"

"No."

"I thought not," he muttered. "Err... can you pass me my bag, please," he said pointing into the kitchen. Christine rolled her eyes at Lenny who was sitting in the armchair, captivated by this intriguing man.

She passed him the bag. "Right. Thanks" he said. He was fondling the sofa arm with the tips of his fingers and then, leaning over, began stroking the cushions. "Mmm," he muttered again. "Can you pass me my bag, please," he repeated.

"It's right next to you.".

"Oh. Right. I'll get on then." He worked his way around the sofa and then began crawling along the carpet parallel with the sofa, humming again. "Right. Where's my bag?" he mumbled, getting up. Lenny and Chris both pointed, restraining an outburst of laughter.

Halibut opened the case, flapping over the large leather strap with a tarnished buckle and rummaging inside. He produced a series of small bags and some tweezers. "Mmm, yes," he repeatedly mumbled as he picked up small hairs and crumbs from the floor and settee. "Clever chap," he said, completing his collection.

"Who?" they asked together with curiosity.

"The man - or woman - who committed this crime. Very clever."

"Why?" they asked.

"Because he - or she - has left very little to go on."

"Doesn't that suggest to you that it might not have been a murder?" asked Leonard, interested.

"Ah. Yes. Possibly," the man retorted looking upset that he may be onto a loser.

"Right. I'll get on..." he continued and paced into the hall. "Where was his jacket exactly?" he called. Chris again got up. She pointed roughly to where Ralph's coat would have laid. The small man lay on his front again, humming.

"His coat - where is it now?"

"In the cupboard, there," she pointed. He moved to a small door under the stairs.

"Which one?" he asked, rummaging.

"That one," she said, leaning over him and touching it.

"Right. I'll get on then." He unhooked the coat and sat on the stairs inspecting it.

He pulled out the bits of paper from the pockets. "My bag... can you bring it here?" he called again. He looked up to find her already offering it to him. "Mmm," he muttered, agitated by her anticipation.

The pieces of paper were all popped into a polythene bag. He then pulled out a jar of powder and a brush and began dusting the front door, on and around the handle and bolts. "Mmm," he muttered and walked through to the kitchen, repeating the exercise on the inside of the back door. "Did you lock the back door yesterday?" he shouted.

"Yes," she replied, standing behind him with his bag.

"Mmm. As I thought. What about the front door, would that have been bolted?"

"I'm not sure. Probably not. He would have left it unbolted so I could get in this morning. Otherwise, if I'd have got home early, I would've had to wake him to get in."

"Wake him?" the man questioned. "How could you have woken him? He was dead, Madam."

"I know but he wouldn't have known that, would he - and nor would I?" she replied, baffled.

"But *would* you?"

"What?"

"How would you have known if he was dead?"

"Eh?"

"If the door was locked..."

"But it wasn't!"

"Mmm. Just as I thought," he muttered, pacing and scratching his head equally confused.

He approached the coffee table and began dusting it.

"What about the television?" he asked. "Was it on?"

"When?"

"When you came in this morning. "

"No."

"Mmm, as I thought." He studied the television set, dusting around the buttons.

"Did he have it on last night?"

"When?"

"When he came in from the pub."

"I don't know. I wasn't here."

"So you wouldn't have known?"

"No. But I think I know!"

"How? If you weren't here, how do you think you know?"

"Because he told me beforehand!"

"Oh?"

"He said he was going to watch the football. But I don't know whether he did..."

"Well you wouldn't, would you?"

"No," she sighed.

"Football you say? At midnight?"

"Yes. A repeat of an earlier game, I think. On the Sports Channel."

" A repeat? My Lord. Do they even repeat football now?" he said, frowning.

He switched on the television which displayed an American Fishing Tournament on the Sports Channel, an American commentator droning with as much excitement as the game itself.

The Cheese Murder

"What did you last see on TV, Miss Ribcage?"

"One of the soaps I think. Yes, last night before I went out to Sockwith," she replied, puzzled.

"Mmm. Just as I thought." He looked around the room again. "Err... the back garden. How do you get to it?"

"The back door!" the couple said together, beginning to laugh quite openly.

"I'm aware of that!" he sniffed irritably. "What I mean, Miss Ribcage, is whether there is another way."

"Oh," she coughed, tensing her face to suppress the laughter. "Yes, you can get round the side."

"As I thought." And he went out the front door humming.

"What a weirdo!" commented Leonard.

"Either he's completely incompetent or there's simply nothing for him to find," said Chris.

"Incriminating evidence, you mean?"

"Yes. He just seems to be getting nowhere. And he's really confusing me. I think he's slightly deranged."

"What was he saying about wellies?" Lenny enquired.

"I don't know. He just asked whether we had any." She paused and smiled: "Listen... can you hear him?"

Halibut was humming loudly in the garden at the rear of the house. Len and Chris broke into laughter once more. Their laughter was so loud they didn't hear him tapping on the kitchen window. He began calling for their attention. Chris eventually heard him and went into the kitchen, still chuckling. "My bag. Can you pass it!" he shouted as she appeared at the window. She retrieved it, still laughing, unlocked the back door and opened it.

"No!" he screamed. "Not the back door!"

"Oh, sorry. I just thought..."

"Oh, very well, pass it to me - but don't step out of the doorway," he instructed.

She stretched her arm out into the cold air, precariously hinged on one leg and passed the bag to the diminutive man standing several yards away.

"Thank you. Now close the door," he ordered. She obeyed,

The Cheese Murder

locking it and returned to Leonard in the lounge.

A few minutes later the man distantly called again. "I say! Can you unlock the door, please?!"

This time Leonard surrendered to his requests, leaving Chris shaking her head, bemused. He went to the back door, turned the key and pushed down the handle.

"Thank you," Halibut sniffed, entering the kitchen and bringing the softening snow in with him. "Right. I'll get on then." And he went into the lounge. He slowly surveyed the sofa once more, gradually reversing towards the fireplace as he pondered, brushing his fizzing chin. The couple stood watching his slow reversal and then peering down at the man's hat behind him on the floor. He reversed further. They looked at each other, grinning and quietly sniggering. Halibut's backward movement, almost in slow motion, finally concluded with his heels crunching onto the hat, half-flattening the round tweed dome, a split opening around the brim. The man kicked his feet up and away from the damage, tutting. He bent down and picked the deer-stalker up, pushing it from the inside in a bid to restore it's shape. The couple innocently looked away.

"Right," he mumbled, humiliated. "I'll get on then." He stroked and fondled his hat as if it were an injured, treasured pet. "Bye."

"Oh. Bye!" Chris replied as he went to the door.

"It's all right now: you can touch everything now. Bye." He walked down the front path, Chris closing the door as he went. She looked at Leonard - and her at him and, in unison, exclaimed "Bag!"

They ran to the back door and opened it. Halibut's tan bag lay half open on it's side in the snow. They stood laughing childishly and watched as the man appeared round the corner of the house, the mutilated hat perched on his head. He noticed them, forced a wry, embarrassed, twisted smile, fumbled the case, shoved it under his arm and muttered: "Right, I'll get on then," the laughing pair simultaneously mouthing his catchphrase.

The Cheese Murder

He trudged off along the side of the house, Leonard and Christine closing the back door, holding each other, giggling.

chapter twelve
murder meetings

Sockwith Police Station was a 1920s, battered, beige painted building in desperate need of repair. An assortment of prefabs stretched across its rear beyond its car park, squeezing up to a scruffy row of muddled tenements. The cracked sign above the main double doors read *"SOCK   LICE STATION"*.

Detective Inspector Brian Fluids and his team were huddled together in 'The Murder Room', an open plan office strewn with desks and pinboards encased in dirt-ridden, creamy gloss walls and rusty old bars at each window, resembling a large prison cell. There were five officers there, all talking at once whilst Fluids was scribbling on a flipchart.

"Right, can we have silence, please?" requested Fluids, clapping for attention. The chattering diminished, heads looked up and he stood, jangling some money in his trouser pocket, rocking back and forth on his heels. "Right then. I've got the report back on Parmesan's Post Mortem. "

"What does it say, Gov?" asked Constable Teeth.

He leant over and picked up a crumpled folder from a rickety table. "Basically, it's sort of inconclusive but there are some serious questions that need answering."

"You mean we don't know whether it was accidental or murder, Gov?" questioned Fledgling, sitting on a table, her slim stockinged legs swinging.

"That's right. As I say, there are a few things that could prove this to be murder."

He swung round to the flipchart and pointed to several words he'd hurriedly written in green marker pen.

"Firstly," he continued, "There's some concern over the cheese and the bread. It appears that there was an unnatural pressure on the roof of his mouth and gums and the top of his oesophagus. There is some doubt over whether Parmesan would have pushed the bread in so hard, no matter how hungry or

The Cheese Murder

inebriated he was." He pointed to the first line of words on the chart: *"Pressure on Pipes"*.

" And what does *Stick* mean?" enquired Stringent, referring to the next line.

"Well, it seems from the contents of Parmesan's stomach that he'd eaten some blue cheese and quite a lot of bread before the killer cheese. The problem is that the amount of bread in his stomach, stuck in his mouth and what was left in the house, adds up to more than he actually bought. How could that be?"

"You mean he must have eaten some other bread on top of what he bought in France?" repeated Stringent requiring clarification, doodling childish creatures on his notepad.

"Yes. And thirdly, Halibut found some bootprints just inside the kitchen door that don't resemble anything worn by the owners of the house - they're around size ten or eleven. Unfortunately, snow had fallen during the night and covered any bootprints in the garden. It's possible that, if it is murder, the killer got in through the back door by poking the key out of the lock from the outside, the key falling onto the floor and then a piece of wire poked under the door to pull it through. Halibut reckons there was a slight scratch on the lino and a patch clear of dust and dirt that could suggest this." He pointed to the last line on the paper: *"The Back Entry"*.

"Oh, right, I get it now!" grinned Stringent stupidly. "I wondered what that all meant!"

"What?" questioned Fluids, puzzled.

"What you wrote, sir: *"Pressure on Pipes Stick the Back Entry"*. I thought it was some sort of..." Everyone was silent.

"Shut up, Stan, for goodness sake!" snapped Teeth.

"So, what we need to do is this," continued Fluids. "We need to find out whether Parmesan actually did have more that three baguettes in the house. Two were untouched in the carrier bag we found in the kitchen, plus virtually a whole stick he had digested, plus the eight inches rammed in his mouth and the bit left over on the table. Stringent, can you do that for me, please? Can you look into it?"

The Cheese Murder

"Yes sir." he replied.

"Secondly, Vivian has already ascertained that there were a few people that had motives for killing him. We need to interview each of these people individually and find out if anyone else qualifies. Teeth, can you do that, please?"

"Yes Gov," he affirmed.

"And Vivian will come with me." He winked at her.

"What about me, sir?" came a whiney voice from the fifth officer.

"Oh, yes, Crumblewick, as you're the new boy, I think you should go with Constable Teeth. Watch and learn, Crumblewick, watch and learn."

"Thank you, sir," he squeaked, looking at Colin Teeth who was mumbling "Why should I have to put up with Crumblewick?"

They buzzed around, getting organised. Fluids clapped authoritatively again and they all dispersed.

Ralph's death had become the single topic of conversation in Larynx. Whilst everyone seemed shocked, no-one was particularly saddened by his demise. The police had so far given nothing away regarding the question of misadventure versus murder. Each villager had his or her own theory, some readily accusing Pierre, having witnessed the outrageous scenes on the France trip. Some quietly wondered about Leonard, others wondered about Christine: perhaps with a secret greed for even greater wealth.

Chris sat in the Blunt Raisin with Leonard having lunch. They were debating whether it was right and proper for Christine to move into Leonard's house so soon after the death - and, more importantly, how the police would view such a move. In reality, the latter was all that held Chris back from immediate departure from 10 Church Lane.

"Give it a few more days, Len. I'll stay over with you and see you during the day, but I'd rather at least appear to be living at Church Lane until the police have finished with me."

The Cheese Murder

"Okay, Giblet. I think that's probably the sensible thing," he replied. He looked at her curiously: "I hope you don't mind me asking, but *you* didn't kill him, did you?"

"Of course not. You know I don't need the money."

"That's what I thought," he confirmed.

"How about you? You didn't do it, did you?" she posed.

"I might have wanted you back, love, but can you see me going to those lengths?" he retorted, smiling.

"Well, it must have been Pierre," she surmised.

After a few seconds it suddenly dawned on her: "Hang on! Oh my God. How could I forget? Clamp! It could have been Clamp!".

"Clamp? Who's he?" asked Lenny mystified. Chris related the story of Ralph's shady threats and blackmail.

"God! I knew nothing of this! He was really mixed up in some heavy stuff, wasn't he!" exclaimed Leonard.

"Yes, Clamp. I think *he* did it!" Chris snapped with real conviction. "Ralph had really got himself into something dodgy there!"

"Have you told the police about this, Chris?"

"Err. No! I forgot!" she said, shocked by her own admission.

"Well we must!" encouraged Lenny. "Try and remember to call them from my house."

They finished their meal and walked together back to Leonard's house. She followed him in, removing her coat and entering the living room. She smiled, viewing the furnishings, decor and ornaments. "I haven't been here for ages, Len. It hasn't changed much, has it?"

"No. Most of this stuff is just as you left it a year ago," he said, picking up a small blue fluffy horse with *"Leonard"* embroidered on its saddle. "Have you still got your one of these?" he asked.

"Yes."

"Pink, wasn't it?" he reflected.

"Yes."

The Cheese Murder

The afternoon brought the couple to the very summit of love and seduction, seizing the opportunity for pleasurable, physical rediscoveries, their thoughts positively distracted from death and accusations.

More serious happenings ensued back at Sockwith Police Station. Fluids and Fledgling were summoned to an urgent meeting in the forensic laboratory with Halibut and the pathologist, James Writhingoose, a man in a white coat and wearing the thickest of round black spectacles, dense lenses protruding like off-cuts from milk bottles. He resembled a mad scientist and had an irritating habit of repeating himself.

"So let me get this straight, Writhingoose," repeated Fluids. "You say that not only had Parmesan eaten around two-thirds of a baguette before the piece stuck in his throat but actually the other third is missing? So there should be the rest of that loaf somewhere?"

Writhingoose nodded.

"Couldn't he have eaten it earlier in the day?" suggested Vivian.

"No. He definitely only ate about two-thirds of a stick prior to dying - and it had only just been digested, only just digested." said Writhingoose.

"And we're certain now," added Halibut "that the killer bread was not Parmesan's at all. The bread was a slightly different sort to that in his stomach."

"You mean the killer brought it with him?" queried Fledgling, sitting bolt upright.

"Yes. The killer bread, although defmitely of French origin, was not one of Parmesan's loaves. Not one of Parmesan's at all," reiterated Writhingoose.

"So," continued Fledgling, scribbling furiously as usual, "the killer is likely to have been someone else on that French trip?"

"Most likely," agreed Halibut.

"Right. The second point I need to fully understand, Halibut," continued Fluids, "is regarding the television. You say

The Cheese Murder

there are definite fingerprints of Ralph Parmesan's on and around the switch, and you confirm that the TV stored the last used channel which was the Sports Channel?"

"Yes."

"Okay. And Ribcage confirmed that she last watched a soap which, presumably would not have been on the Sports Channel?"

"Yes."

"So..." Fluids was still working the process out as he spoke. "This seems to confirm that Parmesan *did* watch the football around midnight when he died."

"That's right," Halibut confirmed, "And the point is, if he was lying on the sofa, watching football and feeling drunk and tired, would he have got up, switched off the TV and then continued eating the food that subsequently caused his death by asphyxiation? It does not make sense, does it? I mean, you would only switch it off once you were ready to go to sleep. It's unlikely that he would continue eating after turning it off, particularly if he was so tired that he slumped into unconsciousness shortly after."

"Mmm. I think I understand your logic, Halibut," frowned Fluids, stroking his rounded chin.

"The other point on this," added Halibut, "is that the lights weren't on in the morning. So, either Parmesan also turned the lounge light off before falling asleep with a face full of food, or he used the light from the television to eat by. With just the light from the dying fire, the victim would have really struggled to see to eat the bread and cheese at all."

"Okay, I'm with you there, Halibut." Fluids looked at Vivian who extracted a new pen from her jacket to complete her scribblings. "Have you got all this so far, Viv?" he asked.

"Yes, sir," she confirmed, massaging her tired writing wrist.

Fluids continued: "The third point you have made to me, then, is regarding the entry point. Yesterday, Halibut, you mentioned a few faint bootprints in the kitchen. Now you say

The Cheese Murder

that you have returned to the garden and found a matching print in the soil under the apple tree where the snow hadn't fallen?"

"That's it. And what's more, a bicycle tyre tread alongside that bootprint. I'm getting some photos of it processed right now. You see, while the snow had covered up 99 per cent of the killer's movements around the side and back of the house, I'm convinced that the bicycle tread and bootprint belonged to him - or her. Also, there was a slight scuff in the bark of the apple tree where the bicycle would have been leant against it." Halibut was smiling proudly as he spoke, thinking back to the way Leonard and Christine had scorned his apparent ineptitude.

"So the killer came into the garden on a bike, wearing boots, and got in the back way?" WPC Fledgling questioned, tapping her exhausted pen on her pad.

"Yes. And he used a piece of wire to poke out the back door key and slide it under the door." Halibut folded his arms in satisfaction.

"The killer, then," Fluids summed up, "came in through the back, up to Parmesan, must have rummaged for his own baguette, taken some cheese from Ralph's plate..."

"No. I think he would have brought his own cheese as well," disputed Halibut. "The killer would not have risked finding Parmesan's cheese, cutting it and... "

"Something else, as well, something else," interjected Writhingoose. "It just so happens that the cheese that blocked the windpipe and primarily caused the suffocation, was a brilliant choice. It's called Mimolette, a sort of Gouda with annatto dye: excellent in terms of texture for effectively cutting off breathing. The other two cheeses that Parmesan had were soft, creamy and crumbly and may not have sealed the windpipe at all. It wouldn't have worked, wouldn't have worked. The killer would not have risked Parmesan having the right sort of cheese for effective suffocation, so he would have brought his own, the Mimolette."

"So the killer brought the bread and the cheese? And he must have taken one of the victim's cheeses as there were still only three there?"

The Cheese Murder

"Yes," the two scientists concurred.

"The killer isn't stupid, then!" commented Fluids. "He's worked this out most carefully. "

"Yes, you may be right," agreed Halibut. "My guess is that the killer is pretty clever - except for one thing..."

"What's that?" Fluids asked, standing and jangling his loose change in his trousers.

"Well, on the carpet we found three bitten fingernails. These nails belong to a male and they're definitely not Parmesan's. We know they were recently deposited there because they were'nt embedded into the carpet pile. These nails could well be the killer's. They need to be matched. "

"Why would he have removed his gloves to bite his nails, for goodness sake?" challenged Fluids.

"Maybe it was a habit. Some people aren't even aware that they're doing it! For instance, he may have nibbled whilst checking the scene before leaving."

Fledgling flicked back through her notes: "So, we need to find out which of our suspects bite their nails, were on the French trip, who wear size ten or 11 Wellingtons and is reasonably intelligent."

"Also," added Halibut, "I think some sort of sheet was used to drape over the body and sofa to protect himself from leaving evidence. A plastic sheet as there are no hairs of threads. There was a distinct lack of evidence left around the victim's head. We would have expected more blood, saliva and breadcrumbs on his neck, chest and clothing. So the killer would have left the scene with a plastic sheet, a piece of bread, a whole chunk of cheese and some wrappers."

"If I could just add, just add," Writhingoose said, "The amount of force used in pushing the bread and cheese into the mouth, although not excessive, is more than one would reasonably accept as self-inflicted. There was also bruising to the right cheek but I think that must have been caused earlier in the day. One more thing as well, I can confirm that his unconscious state was wholly caused by alcohol. No alien drugs

The Cheese Murder

were used by the killer. So it seems the killer must have expected the man to have been in a bad state of inebriation, sufficiently so to have carried out the crime knowing there would little or no struggle. No struggle. "

"And just to complete things," Vivian asked, "the killer would have wrapped up all the bits, locked the back door and then left by the front door?"

"Yes... and probably switching off the TV on his way," Halibut stated.

"This murderer certainly knew Parmesan's moves and plans for that day in pretty good detail!"

Fluids breathed a large sigh. "My word! We've got a lot of work to do here, Vivian!" He stood up and thanked the two men for their efforts.

"Right. I'll get on then," muttered Halibut, packing away his things and reaching for his hat, now half wrapped in thick grey gaffer tape. He scuttled off, humming.

chapter thirteen
the bleach-parsleys

Fifty miles west of Larynx stood a grand Georgian mansion set in ten acres of beautiful, sunlit countryside, its gardens nurtured and maintained by a small team of yokels.

A shiny red Bentley silently glided up the long, winding drive and pulled up outside the huge stone steps. A capped, uniformed driver got out and courteously opened the rear doors. Two figures stepped out. They walked up the steps, between the tall creamy pillars and through a regal, oversized door.

"Yes," the man was saying, "it's a shame the four-poster was beyond repair. Never mind, it's about time we splashed out on a new bed. Perhaps we should go for an even larger, more ostentatious one, Muriel. Maybe one with solid gold patterned inlay on the columns. What do you think?"

"Well why not, dear! I spend enough time staring up at them. It would be quite refreshing to view something else when I'm flat out, dear!"

Muriel was once a fine-looking woman, now in her late fifties. Her hair, unlike her husband's, was her own: golden, full and set firm with spray. Her make-up was slightly excessive, applied in a bid to conceal her ageing wrinkles, crinkles and creases. She wore a thick khaki tweed suit, a clutter of necklaces and rings and pink stilettos which inhibited the sort of deportment associated with dignity. Major Plankton Bleach-Parsley, on the other hand, was relatively straightforward in his attire: a simple, smart grey pin-stripe suit with a flash of red handkerchief and a patterned cotton shirt (one with a plain white collar) which bulged at the neck displaying a thick roll of red paisley cravat. His white moustache curled across his cheeks, resembling a seagull in flight, his conservatively styled wig more yellow than white.

They stood in the large square, tiled hall, a mammoth staircase lined with oil paintings, massive urns and vases holding

The Cheese Murder

columns of pastel dried grasses.

Jilks, the chauffeur, stumbled in, wrestling with bulky carrier bags and a hat box. "Just dump them on the chaise-longue over there, Jilks," directed Muriel.

An old lady, bent at right angles with a hunch-back stumbled into the hall. She wore a royal blue maid's outfit with white braid, the smart clothing contrasting heavily with her deteriorating antiquity. "Excuse me, madam," she said straining her one open eye through a misted up monocle, "there was a telephone call for you."

"Oh?"

"A telephone call..." she repeated, standing right next to the lady of the house, her head level with Muriel's waist.

"Yes? Who was it, Mrs Chaffinch?" Muriel snapped impatiently.

"Oh. I can't remember. Umm... " She reached into a large pocket on the front of her frilly white apron, producing a screwed up tissue. "I wrote it on here... " she fumbled, trying to grin through her few remaining teeth, straining at the handwriting through her monocle.

"Oh get on with it, Chaffinch!" snarled Muriel, hands on hips.

"The Sockly Police... a Constable Strinj or something."

"Sockly?" questioned the woman, looking at Plankton for inspiration. "Where's Sockly for goodness sake?"

"I wrote down the phone number for you, madam," the old lady continued, turning over the tissue and holding it close to her eye, attempting to identify the scratchy blue biro ink.

"Oh give it to me, Chaffinch!" Muriel ordered, snatching the old tissue from the maid. "I can't read this, Chaffinch! Why don't you use the proper paper we have by the telephone. That's what it's there for," she huffed.

"Sorry, Madam. I just happened to be taking it out to wipe my eye when the phone went," she explained, turning away and limping back towards the staff quarters.

"Well hold on, Chaffinch! I need you to decipher this

The Cheese Murder

phone number. I can't make head nor tail of it!"

"Sorry, madam," creaked the maid, turning round and colliding with Jilks who was on his third trip from the car, laden with more bags.

"Chaffinch! Over here, woman!" Mrs Bleach-Parsley called sternly, waving her arms furiously. The Major twisted the old lady into the direction of his wife and she stumbled forward, braking just in time to avoid the meeting of her small head with Muriel's groin.

"Here... Read me the phone number!" ordered the lady, thrusting the tissue underneath the maid's eye. Chaffinch raised her monocle and read it unconvincingly.

"Can you remember that for me, Plankton," requested his wife, pushing the old maid out of her way and walking towards the telephone in the drawing room. Plankton followed, muttering the number repeatedly. She dialled the number.

"Williams' Weasel Farm, good morning," greeted a female on the end of the line.

Muriel crashed down the phone, yelling, " *You stupid old woman. The number's wrong!"*

"Perhaps that tear in the tissue is a number eight not a 6?" replied Chaffinch trying to be helpful.

"Oh never mind! I'll try directory enquiries!" she snarled, lifting the receiver once more and dialling 192. "Hello, I want the number for Sockly Police," she huffed, glaring at the old woman who was still drifting into the room. "What, no Sockly? For goodness sake!" She slammed down the phone again.

"Hold on, Muriel, could it be Sockwith?" contributed Plankton, twirling the wings of his moustache. "You know Sockwith. It's where your son works, isn't it?"

"My son?" she queried.

"Yes, you know... that Ralph chap."

"Oh him. Yes, perhaps it is. Perhaps it's Sockwith," she agreed. "Could it have been Sockwith, Chaffinch?" she asked, leaning down and amplifying her voice into the maid's tiny curled up ear.

The Cheese Murder

"Sockwith? What is?" she grunted, her head shaking stupidly.

"Oh never mind! I'll just try it!" she retorted.

Mrs Chaffinch's closeness to Muriel was irritating her. "Mrs Chaffinch!" she yelled. "Could you move away, please, you're getting your wiry hair on my nice tweed jacket!"

"Eh?"

"Mrs Chaffinch! Go away!!" she ordered, pushing her forcefully. The old maid fell backwards and rolled over onto the large rug, her legs in the air, her skirt falling down to her waist, revealing a pair of off-white bloomers. "Out, Chaffinch! Out!" the lady ordered again. Chaffinch inverted herself onto all-fours and crawled out the room.

"Goodness me, Plankton, why on earth do we keep that wretched old woman on?" she muttered in aggravation.

"I've told you before, dear," he replied. "She's served this family loyally all her life. I can't just discard her, it wouldn't be right."

Muriel tutted and dialled 192 again. "Hello. Yes. I want the number for Sockwith Police."

A digitised voice furnished her with the number and code. She clicked the button on the telephone and immediately dialled.

"Hello? Is that Sockwith Police?... Yes. I wish to speak to a Constable... What was it, Plankton?"

"String, I think. Or was it Strange?" he muttered, scratching his withered temple.

"Constable String or Strange..." she continued. "Well you must have someone with a name something like that? I don't know what it was about, you silly little man! Your lot rang me and left a message with my senile maid!" she fussed. After a long pause, the voice returned to the phone. "Oh at last! They think they might know the name..." she hissed to the Major, "Why are our public services so ruddy incompetent, Plankton?"

He grunted.

"Hello? Who's that I'm speaking to now?" she ordered down the phone. "Strudle? I don't think you're the right man at

The Cheese Murder

all! Strudle sounds nothing like String or Strange, does it? I know you can't help that. Let me explain, Strudle. A Constable telephoned me this morning when I was out. He left a message to call back.... My name? My name is Mrs Muriel Bleach-Parsley... No Parsley, not Parsnip, you silly man."

She huffed and puffed and gritted her teeth. "Look, Strudle," she said trying to calm down, "Could you do something for me, please? Good. Can you find who this man String or Strange is, tell him I rang and get him to call me again. I'll be in until about three o'clock then I'm going out for afternoon tea. Thank you."

She trotted away from the telephone, shaking her head in despair. Her heel crunched on something lying on the rug. "What's this?" she said, bending down. She picked up Chaffinch's monocle, shattered, bent and dangling from a cord, that must have detached itself from its safety pin. "Look, Plankton. Isn't this Chaffinch's eyepiece?"

"Yes," he muttered, taking it from her and inspecting it. "A bit broken, isn't it, dear?" he said in a serious tone. "I'll have to call the optician and see if they can make a duplicate. She'll be lost without this. "

"She's pretty much lost with it!" growled Muriel, striding back into the hall, her officious footsteps echoing around the huge stone walls.

The telephone rang, echoing across the hallway. Mrs Chaffinch appeared. "Madam, that man's on the telephone again for you. Constable Stretcher, I think he said."

"Right. I'll take it in the drawing room."

She lifted the receiver. "Hello? Constable Stretcher is it?"

"Hello Madam. No my name's Constable Stringent. Stan Stringent."

"Well, what can I do for you? Is this something to do with Ralph?"

"Yes, Madam. You're his mother aren't you?"

"Well, yes, I suppose I am," she retorted, reluctant to openly admit her relationship with her son with whom she'd

The Cheese Murder

thoroughly distanced herself.

"Either you are or you're not!" replied Stringent.

"All right! I am!" she said coldly.

"Well, I'm sorry to tell you that something's happened to him," he said evasively.

"I guessed that! You wouldn't have called otherwise, would you?"

"No, you're quite right there," Stan agreed.

"Is it too much to ask what exactly has happened?"

"No, Madam, you can ask me," he replied difficultly.

"Fine. Well, in that case I will. But firstly I would like to ask how on earth you became a policeman when you clearly have less intelligence than Mrs Chaffinch, here." she said pointing to the crotchety old woman who was dusting around the phone.

"Mrs who?"

"For goodness sake! Are you going to tell me about my son or not?!" she shouted, waving her hand in Chaffinch's face, signalling to her to remove her flapping duster from the telephone apparatus.

"Yes, of course," said Stringent apologetically. "But I need to meet you face to face. We're not allowed to explain things like this over the phone."

"Oh! For goodness sake, man! I'm not going to be inconvenienced by waiting for you to come round! Just tell me!"

"I'm not allowed, Madam!"

"Right. Well, if you're not going to tell me, then I'll hang up. I really can't be bothered... "

Stringent sighed with resignation. "All right, I'll tell you. But I shouldn't. It's not the right way..." His voice faded suddenly, preparing to release the news.

"Spit it out, then!" she prompted, hoping for a revelation before having to leave for the tea party. He cleared his throat and muttered quietly: "He's dead," half choking as he broke the news.

"Speak up, man, I can't hear you!"

The Cheese Murder

"He's dead," he repeated, equally inaudibly.

"Shout, man! Shout!" she instructed.

"HE'S DEAD!" he yelled.

"Thank you!" she replied nonchalantly, as if the information was wholly insignificant. "Would you be so kind to tell me how?" she questioned.

"He stopped breathing, madam."

"Well most people do when they die, don't they, officer?" she snorted with further impudence.

"What I mean, madam, is that he suffocated."

"Right. Thank you for telling me. Is that all?"

"Well, we need to meet you to discuss various things and to identify his body."

"Oh," she puffed. "This is most inconvenient. When?"

"Today or tomorrow."

"Very well. I'll come over in the morning. Can you fax me directions to the Police Station?"

"Fax?"

"Yes, fax. I'll give you my number here."

They completed their conversation and Muriel glanced at the large grandfather clock. "Heavens, it's nearly three! Plankton, are you ready?"

"Yes, Muriel." Plankton replied, clattering down the hall. "What did that police chap want?"

"Oh, Ralph's dead" she said, pinning a large gold brooch onto her lapel and studying herself in a tall mirror.

"Oh dear," muttered Plankton. "I'm sorry to hear that, dear."

"Why?"

"He's your flesh and blood, dear," he explained as if it hadn't crossed her mind.

"Well, scientifically, that's true. But that's all. He was a waste. We won't miss him, will we?" She spoke coolly and heartlessly, padding her hair with her hands and applying some bright pink lipstick. "Anyway, I need to go and see those awful police tomorrow and identify his body."

The Cheese Murder

"I'll come with you, dear," he offered sympathetically.

"As you wish, Plankton, as you wish," she said, reaching for her hair spray and blasting it over the top of her head. "Where's Jilks? Is he ready?"

"Here, Ma'am. Your car awaits you," Jilks replied in his deep, deep voice.

The following morning, the Bleach-Parsleys set off for Sockwith. The Major and Muriel sat in the back of the car as usual. He respectfully wore black, she wore cerise. The car entered Sockwith: the bridge over the wide canal, red-brick rows of houses, old grey ramshackle offices.

"What an awful place," Muriel muttered in disgust as they approached the town centre. "No character at all. Just look, Plankton: not a single boutique, not a single quality department store, just the normal run-of-the-mill mediocrity... Come on Jilks, what's the delay?"

"Road works, Ma'am."

She tutted impatiently and watched a man holding a manual "Stop Go" disc who seemed to keep it permanently on "Stop". She huffed, tutted and eventually pressed the button to descend her window. "Excuse me, lad!" she called. "Would you mind revolving that ruddy sign?"

"In a minute, lady," he snorted. He continued to stand motionless.

"Are there any cars approaching, Jilks?" she asked, peering over his shoulder.

"No, Ma'am."

"Oh, come on laddy," she shouted aggressively. "Turn your silly little lollipop thing round, could you?"

"In a minute, lady. Keep your hair on!" he shouted.

"He's playing games now," she muttered as he teased her by turning the sign a quarter of the way and then turning it back to red.

"Jilks, if it's clear, put your foot down, will you?" she ordered, fuming at her treatment by the Sockwith Corporation

The Cheese Murder

Highways worker.

"Right you are, Ma'am," he responded. The car screeched, the wheels spun and it launched itself wildly past the sign controller in a blast of smoke.

"I'm reporting you to the authorities!" she yelled out the window, waving her index finger violently as they accelerated.

"Look out, Jilks, old chap!" called Plankton, noticing an old man cycling towards them along the narrow stretch of road. The car swerved to the left, the bicycle to the right. Jilks expertly negotiated a series of potholes and traffic cones. Plankton looked out the rear window to witness the veteran cyclist sprawled across a flattened roadworks sign, his legs entangled in the bicycle chain.

"Ruddy road works! They're a danger to society!" muttered Muriel. "Is it much further, Jilks?"

"No, Ma'am, it's just around the corner." The car turned left, Jilks slowed it down and drove it into a small visitors' car park.

"What a hideous place!" she commented as Jilks opened her door.

The Bleach-Parsleys walked round to the front. She noticed the sign reading *SOCK LICE STATION,* grimaced nauseously and followed the Major into the building.

"Major and Mrs Bleach-Parsley," he introduced to an officer at the front desk. "We're here to see a Constable Stringent."

"Please take a seat," gestured the man, lifting the phone.

"Don't sit down, Plankton, you don't know what filth might be lurking," she instructed, referring to the row of old wooden chairs with green hairy woollen covers. They stood around for five minutes. Stan Stringent appeared at a door.

"Mrs Bleach-Parsley?" he asked a decrepit woman sitting at the opposite end of the waiting room.

"Over here, man!" called Muriel.

"Oh. I'm sorry, Madam," he smirked. "Would you like to come through?" He opened the door for her politely. Plankton

The Cheese Murder

followed. Stan Stringent directed them down the corridor and into the large investigation room where a few officers sat around looking vaguely occupied. The large sign, *Murder Room* swung from the ceiling, helpfully reminding the officers of their purpose.

"Over here, please," he ushered and they went into a small interview room.

"Why are we in the Murder Room?" questioned Muriel.

"Ralph was murdered," replied Stan. "Didn't I tell you that?"

Vivian Fledgling came in. "Good morning, I'm Detective Constable Fledgling," she said, smiling softly and shaking their hands. "Would you like a cup of tea?"

"Yes, that would be..." began Plankton.

"No, we won't, thank you!" interrupted Muriel, disgusted by the lack of cleanliness of the entire establishment.

"Thanks for coming. I'm sorry about your son's death. I hope we can wrap everything up quickly," continued Fledgling.

"Do you know who murdered him?" asked Plankton with consternation, fiddling again with his moustache.

"No, I'm afraid not." Fledgling replied.

Stringent added, "The problem is that everyone hated the chap, so we're having to interview heaps of people..."

Vivian coughed and continued: "What my colleague means is..."

"Don't worry, dear," Muriel interjected, "You don't have to cover up for him. I'm well aware Ralph was a nasty piece of work. Don't try and make out he was an angel for my sake." She smiled back at the WPC, sympathetically.

"Well, you said it, lady!" commented Stringent. "He was in all sorts of trouble. You're right: he was a nasty, nasty, nasty man!"

"All right, Stan. That's enough!" whispered Vivian sternly. "Now, as you can understand, we need to interview everyone connected with this case," she explained. "It appears there may be a number of motives. We need to ascertain whether there are

The Cheese Murder

any more likely candidates and establish where everyone was when it happened. It's not that we suspect you but I'm sure you understand we need to ask. And, of course, you are his parents so .. "

"I'm not his parent!" the Major butted in. "I'm his step-father. His real father died some years ago."

"Oh, I'm sorry" said Fledgling, flicking through some typewritten notes. "Yes, of course," she continued, finding the appropriate text, "The Reverend Parmesan died four years ago... Oh, it doesn't say how he died..."

"Does it matter?" questioned Muriel, writhing on her hard seat.

"Well no. We're not here for that, are we?" apologised Fledgling. "Can I ask you, then, what you were both doing around midnight on Tuesday?"

"Tuesday..." muttered Plankton. He looked at his wife who looked briefly embarrassed. "Oh, yes," he grinned, Muriel's expression triggering his memory. "We were in bed. Err ... we were... ummm." He didn't know quite how to explain himself.

He nervously tugged at his creamy moustache, pulling the ends down below his chin. He coughed. "I remember it well," he continued, still struggling, "the four poster broke during err..."

"You've got a four poster bed?" Stringent questioned childishly.

"Err, yes," replied Plankton, still molesting the thick facial fur.

"And you broke it?" he grinned.

"Umm."

"Wow! You two must be pretty wild!" he exclaimed, glowing. Fledgling kicked him under the table.

"Can anyone verify your whereabouts?" she asked with her usual professionalism.

"Well, Chaffinch and Jilks both live in. But I don't know whether they would be able to absolutely confirm it," explained the Major.

"They might have heard the noise!" Stringent suggested,

The Cheese Murder

trying to help.

"Well, you'll have to ask them, won't you?" replied Plankton uncomfortably.

"How did you get on with Ralph, Mrs Bleach-Parsley?" asked Vivian.

"I didn't. Ralph left home many years ago. He never approved of me and the Major. He doted on his dad," she said.

"I see. And when did you last see Ralph?"

"At his father's funeral. I've not set eyes on him since. He made it quite clear he didn't want anything to do with us."

"Now he's dead, what are you going to get out of it?" asked Stan Stringent bluntly. The couple looked at each other. "Absolutely nothing!" they both said.

"I don't even know if I'm next of kin or whether he's married or..." continued Muriel.

"Fine," concluded Vivian. "That's all we need to ask, really. Now all we need you to do, Mrs Bleach-Parsley, is to get you to identify Ralph, if you would."

"All right. But I'm not sure if I remember him."

"I'm sure you'll recognise him if it is your son. Please, can you come with me? Major, would you mind going with PC Stringent? He'll take you to back to reception."

They all stood up and paired off.

Vivian accompanied Ralph's mother along a labyrinth of corridors and stairways, finally arriving at a white tiled room.

"Now, all you need to do is to take a look at his face and then tell me whether it's Ralph or not," she whispered. "Another person will be present to witness this."

She put her arm around Muriel. Muriel nodded and slowly walked further into the room. The clinical apparatus and lack of decor produced an eery, morbid atmosphere, even for someone as icy as Muriel Bleach-Parsley. A man in a white coat pulled open a large metal drawer.

"Are you ready?" asked Vivian quietly, holding her hand.

Muriel nodded. They stepped up to the drawer. The man carefully gripped the two corners of a white sheet that covered

The Cheese Murder

the body's head. He slowly pulled back the cover revealing the features: hair, eyes, nose, mouth and cheeks, chin, throat.

"That's a woman!" gasped Muriel in shock. The man immediately heaved the drawer back.

"Who's *this* then, Constable?" asked the mortuary attendant, clearly confused.

"This is *Ralph Parmesan's* mother," Vivian replied through gritted teeth. "I'm sorry, Mrs Bleach-Parsley. He must have been expecting someone else for another identification."

Muriel straightened her suit and cleared her throat. "Come on, get on with it, " she urged, disturbed by the turn of events and wishing to leave.

The man studied his notes and moved to another drawer. "Right," he said.

"You're Ralph Parmesan's mother, yes?" he asked for absolute confirmation.

"Yes, Yes!" snapped Muriel. "Get on with it, for goodness sake!"

He pulled strongly at the drawer and hurriedly flung back the sheet. Muriel looked down. It was Ralph all right. His thick chunk of rough, ruffled, unstyled hair still topped his head as it had throughout his childhood. His hard expression had gone, presumably, she thought, because his aggressive facial muscles were now inactive. His skin looked quite smooth as if he'd shaved in preparation for her visit. She noticed odd speckles of powder around his thin pinkish mouth.

"What's that?" she asked, pointing close to the corners of his lips.

"Oh, it's a powder we use. Just make-up, really," explained the man vaguely, not wishing to detail the reason Ralph's lips had cracked.

"Well, it's certainly him," she said turning away and moving towards the door.

The drawer slammed as she left.

"Thank you, Mrs Bleach-Parsley. Are you okay?" asked Fledgling.

The Cheese Murder

"Oh yes, I'm fine!" she replied. The sight of her son had little effect. If anything, it had surfaced all her worst feelings for the man, rather than any pleasant sentiment.

"How did he die exactly?" she asked curiously, in a tone one might use when enquiring about a new style of hat.

"Someone suffocated him," Fledgling replied as they retraced their steps to the front of the building.

"What? With a pillow or something?"

"Err. No. Not a pillow... " Fledgling was reluctant to elaborate.

"What then? You can tell me!"

"Well, he was drunk. Flat out drunk... " Fledgling began.

"That doesn't surprise me in the least!" snorted Muriel.

"And..." continued the Constable, "it seems that whoever killed him did so by forcing a lump of cheese into his throat, pressing it right down with a length of french bread. It was the cheese that did it. It cut off his breathing, you see."

Muriel started to laugh. "Oh my God! Only Ralph could die like that! Well, whoever did it, did it in style, I'll say that for them!" she joked.

They continued walking down the long bare corridors. "Did Ralph have anyone? I mean, did he have a girlfriend or a wife - or even a boyfriend?"

"Yes," Fledgling replied, "he was living with a girl. They were due to marry in January."

"Oh, really? Someone trying to make an honest man of him?!" exclaimed Muriel in surprise.

"Well," explained Vivian, "Actually they'd just split up last weekend and were about to cancel the wedding. It was a mutual decision, I believe. I think Christine's gone back to an old boyfriend."

"Christine?"

"Yes, that's her name, Christine Ribcage."

The name meant nothing to Muriel. Ralph could have been married with twenty children for all she knew.

"I think I might go to Larynx. What's she like, this

The Cheese Murder

Christine? A likeable sort?"

"Yes, I think so. I don't really know her. I'm going down to Larynx myself now."

"I may see you there then."

They approached Plankton, seated in the waiting room.

"Plankton, really!" Muriel scolded.

"What, dear?"

"You're sitting on one of those awful woolly chairs. I told you not to! We'll probably have to disinfect you now!"

The Cheese Murder

chapter fourteen
press and impressionists

The police were now a permanent fixture in Larynx. Every minute of the past few days the villagers had caught sight of a police car, a uniformed officer or the glow of a blue flashing light. The general Christmas mood and festivities had been somewhat nullified by the recent events.

Larynx was also playing host to a squad of press and TV journalists. Brian Fluids' team were all working flat out, with the Chief Inspector, Fledgling and Stringent now at number ten Church Lane once more.

Fluids, outside the house, was answering questions from the press and giving a well-rehearsed statement to the TV crews. Stringent stood about in the background ensuring that his presence was likely to be caught on camera. Leonard and Christine had planned to start transferring some of her more vital belongings to Cobblestone Street but the amount of attention and visibility her house was receiving persuaded her to keep well clear.

The red Bentley pulled into the village. Plankton was pointing straight down the road to the bustle outside Ralph's house.

"That must be the house, dear."

"Pull up here, Jilks," ordered Muriel and the car drew up outside the general store. "Wait here, Jilks. Come on, Plankton, we'll walk. Let's see what these nosey people are up to."

She approached the TV crews and pressmen, barging through the crowd, causing a fourth take of Fluids' filmed interview. Stringent stopped them: "Hello, Mrs Bleach-Parsley. I didn't expect to see you here."

A tatty journalist behind the officer stuck his head forward. "Who's this then?" he asked, thrusting a small dictating machine into Stringent's face.

"This is the victim's mother, Mrs Bleach-Parsley,"

announced Stringent loudly, feeling important that he'd revealed something new to the press. Upon hearing this, the rest of the media crowd swerved round, their attention drawn away from Fluids and his formal speech. The 15 or so people swamped Ralph's mother, firing noisy questions, scrapping to get closest.

"Get away, you horrible little vultures!" she stormed. "I have no desire to speak to you lot!"

The press, after a moment's reactionary pause, recommenced their noisy interrogations. "How do you feel about the murder?" one shouted. "Were you close to Parrnesan?" cried another. "Tell us about your sex life!" yelled another.

"Well, really!" she snorted. "You vile animals! Isn't there anyone here from a quality broadsheet?"

A smartly dressed man barged through. "I'm from the Telegraph. I shall be pleased to speak to you privately," he called. The riff-raff element took exception to this and pushed forward rebelliously.

In the mêlée, one reporter's camera, held above head-height scraped the top of the Major's head, the base of the flashgun hooking onto his yellowing wig. The camera was lifted, round hairpiece attached, resembling a small fluffy toilet seat cover. The scuffle continued, Plankton waving his hands frantically in the air trying to retrieve his hairpiece. In the commotion, the camera suddenly jerked, catapulting the wig above and over the crowd into the road, landing on an open drain.

Plankton squeezed his way out of the throng in pursuit. He saw it perched flatly between two of the drain's grilles, water from melted snow gurgling its way from the gutter into the dark abyss. The barging continued and one reporter was propelled backwards, his shoe scraping on the drain as Plankton was bending down. As the man steadied himself, removing his foot and pushing forward once more, Plankton looked down to find the circle of hair now dangling precariously into the drain, only resisting its complete descent with the assistance of a piece of grey twisted chewing gum. Plankton bent down again, two

The Cheese Murder

fingers posing like pincers, concentrating on the sticky chunk that had prevented its departure into the sewer system. He slowly and gently gripped the lump of gum, which acted as a reliable handle, and lifted, threading the main bulk of wig up between the grilles. He breathed a sigh of relief, rolled up his treasured toupée, complete with dirt, water and gum and poked it into an inside pocket.

Mrs Bleach-Parsley was still resisting interview. WPC Fledgling had intervened in the commotion, repelling the surging journalists.

"I want my husband!" Muriel pleaded to her, the episode starting to take its toll, tears beginning to blot on her thickly powdered face.

"Major!" called Vivian, "Major?!" looking desperately for the man. The journalists, hearing his title, heaved towards him some yards away as he silently stood wiping his hands on a large paisley handkerchief. Suddenly the throng was upon him crying "Major! Major!"

"Just push off!" he shouted, turning his back on them and pacing down the road.

The group gave chase.

"If I were you I'd leave, Mrs Bleach-Parsley. Give it a few days for things to die down," shouted Fledgling above the din. Muriel nodded, stunned by this outrageous behaviour. Plankton was hot-footing it full circle back towards the church, the wild crowd splashing and sploshing in the slush as they tailed him. Vivian grabbed Muriel's arm and rushed her to the car. Jilks flung open both the rear doors. Plankton leapt in one side, Muriel the other, both flustered and dishevelled. Jilks turned the key and depressed the accelerator, driving straight into the crowd, reporters hurling themselves into bushes to safety.

At the far end of the village, away from the frantic scenes of the ravenous media, two officers had arrived at a pretty, tidy cottage. PC Colin Teeth and the novice, PC Crumblewick, walked up the neat garden and knocked on the door. A net

The Cheese Murder

curtain twitched in the window and a small head appeared. The door opened.

"Hello. Mrs LePants?" enquired Teeth.

"Yes," confirmed the petite woman.

"Do you mind if we come in and ask a few questions?" Teeth continued, stepping forward.

"Come in," she said, holding the door open. "Please wipe your feet." The two policeman complied. "Come in here," she said, walking into a large, airy living room, paintings adorning every wall. "Is this to do with Ralph Parmesan?" she asked, sitting, small legs together, hands on knees.

"Yes," replied Teeth, removing his helmet.

"Please, sit down," she requested, pointing to a large soft sofa. Teeth sat.

Crumblewick was standing, looking round the room.

"What a lovely room, Mrs Pants," he admired. "These paintings... Impressionist, aren't they?"

"Yes. French Impressionist," she confirmed. Crumblewick moved from picture to picture, positively glowing.

"These are beautiful prints - and so nicely framed!" he commended. "I recognise the Cezanne, the group of Renoirs and this lovely Pissarro," he continued, studying the full size print of the *Place du Theatre Francais, Paris.*

"But what's this one?" he said, peering deep into the thick reds, creams and blues. "This picture has such life and vibrancy!"

"It's a Monet. *Rue Montoguiel Decked With Flags,* it's called" she said.

"A Monet? Never!" he exclaimed. "I've never seen one of his like this before!"

"It's reputed to be his best piece of work. It's a painting of the peace celebrations held on June 30th 1878 at the opening of the Universal Exposition," she said expertly.

"Really quite sensational!" he breathed.

Teeth sat bored and agitated.

"Crumblewick! Much that you seem to be enjoying this, I

think we ought not detain Mrs LePants longer than we have to! Come and sit down!"

"It's all right, Constable. It's pleasing to see someone with a clear interest in art," Pandora remarked.

Crumblewick sat, still gazing at the array of pictures. The dining room was partitioned from the front room by means of a set of glazed doors. Further groups of framed prints hung majestically on the far walls. He strained his eyes, trying to identify them. Teeth nudged him.

"Right, Mrs LePants..." began Teeth.

"Please, call me Pandora, it's so much nicer!" she interrupted.

"Oh. Right, Pandora. Presumably your husband's at work, is he?"

"Yes. He'll be back around six-thirty."

"Well," Teeth continued, "although we need to see him, I'd like to ask you some questions as well. Firstly, can you tell me where your husband and yourself were around midnight on Tuesday?"

"Tuesday? Two days ago?" she muttered. "Well we would have both been asleep. Yes. That was the day of the trip to Calais. We were both very tired and went to bed early, about 10:30."

"Are you sure that Pierre was in bed with you around midnight?" Teeth enquired.

"Yes, we were both asleep."

"But can you confirm that he was actually there with you, at midnight?" he repeated with extra clarity.

"Well, I'm sure I would have awoken if he'd got up, if that's what you mean. I always wake up if he goes to the loo in the night or whatever," she replied. Crumblewick was writing.

"I know what you're getting at, officer," she continued. "You know about the altercation in the hypermarket between Ralph and Pierre that day?"

"Yes, we do know that," nodded Teeth. "Do you know what it was about?" he asked tactfully, not wishing to reveal this

The Cheese Murder

information if she affirmed her ignorance.

"No I don't," she said. "They'd been getting at each other for a while. I can only assume that Ralph was winding him up because he was an ex-boyfriend of Christine's."

"Well, it's more than that, Pandora, I'm afraid. But I feel that I shouldn't be the one to tell you. If anyone should, it should be Pierre," he advised sensitively.

"Oh. Right" she muttered, worry spreading across her tiny face.

"I wouldn't worry too much. Now that Parmesan's dead, I don't think it matters anyway. Don't get too worked up about it." His intention was to reassure and console her.

"But presumably that's the whole issue?" she challenged with consternation. "You clearly think Pierre had a pretty good reason to get Ralph out the way, yes? You just said that now he's dead, the matter's resolved!"

"Well, we'll see, Pandora. But please don't worry. It's early days yet. Pierre's no more a suspect than anyone else."

"But he *is* a suspect, yes?" she continued bravely.

"Yes, I'm afraid he is but so are others. Parmesan was not well liked. Anyway, can you answer a few more questions that may help your husband?"

"Yes, of course," she said, still showing deep concern.

"Can you tell me what size shoes he takes?"

"Ten or 11. It varies," she replied.

"And does he own any Wellington boots?"

"Yes he does. He's a keen gardener, you see."

"Sorry to ask you, Pandora, but can we borrow them, please?" Teeth requested almost with profound regret. This lady was courteous, pleasant and clearly intelligent. Both officers found it hard to question such an amiable person, particularly when she may be incriminating her husband with every word.

Pandora scuttled out of the room, calling "They're in the kitchen. He keeps them there ready for his gardening."

The two Constables were silent in her absence, Crumblewick again strolling round the framed prints, Teeth

The Cheese Murder

sitting unoccupied.

Pandora returned after a minute or so, clean, shiny boots in hand. She handed them to Crumblewick.

"I'll get you a bag for them."

Teeth tried to conceal his disappointment over the revelations of Pierre's shoe size and possession of boots. This evidence could make or break their suspicion and, presently, he feared the worst. But he had to continue his officious questioning: "You say you both went to France on the minibus on Tuesday?"

"Yes."

"Where was Ralph? Was he close to you both on the bus?"

"Yes, he was right behind us. He was being a real nuisance. He was continually winding up Pierre, causing great annoyance. He was loud and irritating."

"Was he threatening?"

"Well, no, not at that stage. But something was going on. He seemed to know that he could really annoy Pierre and get away with it. He kept saying: 'Ill tell your wife!' Pierre took a lot of abuse that day."

"Can *I* ask something?" interrupted Crumblewick, feeling somewhat redundant. "Do you know who, on the trip, would have known what Ralph was going to buy - you know, bread and cheese?"

Teeth looked at him slightly mystified but Crumblewick gave the impression his question was wholly relevant. The diminutive Pandora sat, sunk deep in her armchair and thought.

"Actually," she said, having fully reflected on the outing, "I remember that the group on the back seat each announced what they were proposing to buy. Ralph had been particularly coarse, loud enough for everyone on the bus to know."

"So he mentioned baguettes and cheese?" queried Crumblewick.

"Yes. And as I say, he yelled it out. He shouted something like: 'I'm going to get a load of french sticks, cheese and beer, go down the pub when I get back, get legless, and then go home

The Cheese Murder

and fill my face with the food'. Something like that, anyway. I don't think he said 'legless', though," she blushed. "Oh... and he said he was going to watch the football on TV after the pub."

The officers looked at each other.

"So," continued Crumblewick, "what you're saying is that everyone on the bus would have heard this, so they would have all known his plans?"

"Oh yes. He really yelled it out."

"Can I ask something else?" asked Crumblewick excitedly. "What did you and your husband buy at Mammouth?"

"Oh, quite a lot of wine, that's all. Pierre loves his wine. He says its so expensive over here and the choice is pretty limited."

"True, true," agreed Crumblewick. He felt a strong affinity with this lady.

"Do you have the receipt for the wine?" he asked.

"I don't know... " she answered, getting up. "I suppose Pierre may have put it in the drawer in the dining room. That's where we put all our receipts."

She slid back the glass door. Crumblewick arose. He followed her in, excited at the prospect of viewing more prints. "My word, Pandora," he drooled, "these pictures are fantastic, and so well presented."

"Thank you. I mount and frame them myself," she said whilst flicking through a pile of receipts.

"Gaugin, Van Gogh, more Van Gogh ... oh and my favourite: *The Canoe* by Georges Seurat! It's just so ... so .. *Impressionist!"* he beamed. He continued looking round the room. A wine rack stood in the corner by the window, virtually full from floor to ceiling.

"My word! I see what you mean about French wines!" exclaimed Crumblewick sliding bottles in and out. Bottles of Brouilly, Chiroubles, St-Emilion, Moulis, Bourgogne Chardonnays, rows of Chablis 1987s, rows of reds and whites from Provence and a whole stack of the familiar Chateauneuf-du-Pape.

"Here we are," she said and passed a receipt to the officer.

The Cheese Murder

He studied it and took it back into the front room, showing it to Teeth. The receipt listed nothing but wine: detailing the name and volume of each type purchased.

"Thank you, Pandora," said Teeth, standing. "You've been really helpful. We won't keep you any longer."

"Yes, thank you, Pandora, " repeated Crumblewick, shaking her minute hand affectionately. "You really have a splendid home - real taste!" he smiled. "Bye then, I hope to see you again soon!" he waved, moving towards the door carrying the carrier bag containing the wellies.

The Cheese Murder

chapter fifteen
pub and passion

Darkness had fallen on Larynx. The media crews had departed with only a little gossip to reap across the nation. Teeth and Crumblewick had driven back to Sockwith to meet Halibut to see if Pierre's Wellington boots matched the print.

Fluids, Stringent and the WPC concluded their house-to-house enquiries in Larynx for the day.

"Right, Stan, you can get off now. I think we've done enough for today," directed his superior.

"Oh, good!" smiled Stringent. "I might be able to get home to video the national and regional news: see if you're on it!" He really hoped that he could catch himself on screen. "Bye!" he called trudging to his car.

Fluids and Fledgling stood rubbing their hands in the cold.

"Well, Viv, it's nearly six. I'm starving. Do you fancy a bit of nosh while we're here?" he asked.

"Oh!" She was taken by surprise. She'd never really socialised with the Inspector.

"Come on, Viv. A stiff brandy would probably do us both good as well," he smiled, starting to walk. She didn't move. She was still unsure. "Besides," he called, arriving at the car, "there's also a few other reasons I have for getting you alone."

"Oh? Like what?" she asked curiously, beginning to follow.

"I'll tell you later!" he teased.

"Okay. But I'm in my uniform, sir. Do you mind if I take the car and go home to change first? I don't like sitting in pubs in uniform. I look so conspicuous."

"Of, course! I tell you what, I'll meet you at the Blunt Raisin in, say, an hour?"

"Right, sir," she said, walking hastily to the car outside St Barnaby's.

Brian Fluids walked the short distance to the Blunt Raisin. He entered, the landlord greeting him at the bar.

The Cheese Murder

"Evening, sir. You're the Detective on the Parmesan case aren't you?" asked Jim.

Fluids nodded.

"Well, what can I get you?"

"Double Courvoisier, please. You knew Ralph Parmesan then?" leaning on the bar, a folded twenty pound note in his hand.

"Oh yes, sir. I knew him. Not well, but I knew him. I always dreaded him coming in here." He spoke with his back to Brian whilst pushing a large bowl-shaped glass up to the optic. He turned, placing the liquor on the beer mat in front of Fluids. He took the money, still talking: "Yes, he was always loud and unruly. Most of the time he wasn't even with anyone. He'd just sit alone at the bar, drink heavily and eventually get abusive."

"Didn't you ever bar him?" asked Fluids, taking his change.

"No. I used to warn him but on most occasions he'd just finish his drink and go elsewhere. Then I wouldn't see him for days - or weeks, sometimes. Then he'd reappear and we'd go through the routine once more. I reckon this probably happened in all the. I know the Grinning Plank was particularly tolerant with him."

"Was he always that bad, drunk and unruly?" Fluids enquired, finding it hard to believe. He sat on a bar stool wrapped in his long raincoat, slowly sipping his Cognac.

"Yes. Always. Except his last visit when I must say, he was quite gentlemanly by his standards."

"Really? When was that?"

"Last Sunday. He came in with Christine, his girlfriend, for Sunday lunch."

"Really?" he asked, this new information brightening his expression. "What can you tell me about it?"

"Well, not a lot." Jim occasionally wiped the bar during the conversation, as if nervous at his own candour. "They came in here dead on twelve. Chris ordered them both a drink and gave me her credit card to set up a tab. They sat over there on the sofa," he said, pointing towards the roaring, glittering fire.

The Cheese Murder

"Parmesan came up to the bar a few times to refill his glass..."

"Lager?"

"Yes. Then, about half-twelve, they went up there to the dining area and had their meal."

"Did they come here often to eat?"

"Oh, no! I think this may well have been the first time. I was quite surprised when Christine said they were going to eat here!"

"So, presumably a special occasion of some sort?" Fluids concluded, his interest deepening.

"I don't know. The waiter or waitress that served them may be able to help you there. They probably had more chance of overhearing them than me. All I can say is that they seemed perfectly at ease with each other; no raised voices or anything."

The Detective Inspector rubbed his glass in deep thought. "You couldn't do me a favour, could you?" he asked.

"I'll see if I can find out which staff served them for you, if that's what you're asking," he smiled.

"I'm most grateful," smiled Fluids, extending his hand in thanks. "My name's Brian Fluids, by the way."

"Jim. Jim Basin," he replied, shaking the man's hand. 'I'll see if I can get them for you."

He walked out the back of the bar towards the kitchen. Fluids delved his hand under his raincoat and into his jacket pocket, pulling out a note pad and pen. He sat silently for a while, scribbling. The warmth from the open fire across the room caused the man to remove his coat. He folded it and placed it on the stool next to him.

"I've managed to find the two who served them last Sunday. Fortunately they're both working tonight," Basin announced. "They'll pop over when they've got a moment."

"Thanks, Jim."

DI Fluids checked his watch and looked towards the door each time a customer entered, anticipating Vivian Fledgling's company. Ten minutes passed before a waiter and waitress approached.

The Cheese Murder

"Ah. You're the two that served Parmesan and his girlfriend last Sunday lunchtime?" he smiled, twisting round on his stool. They nodded nervously, like schoolchildren in trouble. "Can either of you tell me what they were talking about?"

"Well, sir," said the girl, half curtseying as she spoke, "All I could gather was that they were discussing their relationship and that it wasn't really getting anywhere. That's all I heard, really."

"All I heard," added the male, "was that they had agreed to split up."

"Is that all you heard?" Fluids asked, disappointed.

"Yes, sir," they said in unison.

"There was no row, no insults, no abuse?"

"No sir," they said.

"Nothing more to add? Nothing strange happened? Nothing you think was out of the norm?" the Inspector continued.

"No sir." said the man.

"Well, sir... " muttered the girl, bowing. "There was something I thought a bit strange but probably not..."

"Go on," encouraged Fluids, hopes rising.

"Well, the man..."

"Yes? Yes?"

"He wanted Thousand Island Dressing with his garlic mushrooms," she said, almost embarrassed at the triviality of her statement.

"Mmm," grunted Fluids, deflated. "That's it?"

"Yes sir."

"Okay, you two. Thanks. You can go now," he muttered, turning back towards the bar and his drink.

The girl then reversed and tapped him on the shoulder. "Sorry, sir. But I've just remembered something else. I don't know whether it's any use or..."

"Go on," mumbled Fluids keeping his back to her, expecting the worst.

"Well, I remember now. When they were first talking,

The Cheese Murder

before they went over to eat, he was saying something about threatening his boss with the papers over something or other. Something to do with a death of someone or other." She then turned away as if her information was as irrelevant as the Thousand Island sauce. Fluids swivelled round and grabbed her arm.

"Wait!" he ordered. "This death: did he mention a name?"

"Err, yes, I think so. But I can't remember..."

"Archie? Was the man's name Archie? Archie Pond?" he prompted.

"Yes! That's it!" she replied, smiling and curtseying furiously.

"What else did he say to her about it?" he pleaded, jerking her arm excitedly. "Think carefully! Think really hard! What else? Words, names, anything!"

She stood silently, head bowed, eyes screwed up, thinking with all her might. Fluids was squeezing and squeezing her arm. The more he squeezed the harder she thought. Then she lifted her head, illuminated, and opened her mouth, Fluids shaking her.

"Factory!" she grinned. "Yes, a factory!"

"What do you mean, a factory?" hustled the Inspector, his good looks turning demonic in frustration.

"That was it! A factory!" she beamed.

"I don't understand!" Fluids knew the climax to this revelation was imminent. But this girl was prolonging the agony to the extent where his self-control was beginning to crumble. "Explain! Explain what you mean! Please!"

"Well," she said slowly, trying to arrange the most concise series of words: anything to stop him puncturing every blood vessel in her arm. "What I mean is this.... "

"Yes?!" he urged again, gripping her with more brute force.

"He was saying something about..." She stopped again, screwing up her face to extract her vague memories.

"Yes?!"

"He was going to go to the press," she started, eyes now looking up to the heavens for assistance, "about how his boss

The Cheese Murder

had something to do with that man's death..."

"Archie's, yes, and ..?"

"... and that he was going to tell the papers about his... his 'sordid' – yes, that was the word, 'sordid past' at a factory. He said that, because of this, he'd got himself a pay rise and... there was something else the boss had promised him... a bus... a new bus? Something like that."

Fluids released her arm and the girl flopped back to normality after the minutes of pain, strain and effort.

"Right," he sighed. "So, let me get this straight. You reckon you heard Parmesan saying to his girlfriend that he was blackmailing his boss into keeping his job and getting a new bus. The threat was to expose the boss for his part in Archie's death and for something sordid he'd done in a factory? Is that it?"

"Mmm," she replied. It sounded so ridiculous she turned red with embarrassment while rubbing her bruised arm. "That's what I heard, sir, sorry." She curtseyed again . "I know it sounds a bit..."

"No, no, not at all!" he replied with congratulation. "It makes perfect sense, my dear." He patted her on the shoulder.

"Oh. Good. Thank you sir. Can I go now?" She nodded and bowed, still grasping her dented, red arm.

"Of course. Thank you err..."

"Trish."

"Thank you, Trish. You've been most helpful. Sorry about your arm, by the way," he called as she hurried away from him into the back. He excitedly opened his notebook and jotted the notes down furiously.

"Hello, sir, sorry I'm late," came Vivian's voice.

"Oh, hi, Viv. Drink?" he said, smiling. "Good Heavens!"

"What?"

"Don't you look different out of uniform!" he exclaimed in delight. Her black hair curled loosely down to her shoulders. Her white jumper clung to her body, the curves of her generous chest stretching the stitching. She wore tight, cropped pale blue jeans that similarly hugged every contour. The irresistible cuddliness

The Cheese Murder

of her top half became an irresistible grabbableness around her lower half. As she leant over the bar, peering at the range of optics, Fluids' hands twitched with an compulsion to slap both beautifully contained buttocks. Her legs had always been a great attraction to him in their black tights. But her jeans took nothing away: they looked equally ravishing wrapped in taut, crease-free denim. A hint of pink cotton sock appeared at the hem, vanishing into a pair of fur-rimmed suede boots.

"What was that?" he asked, acknowledging her reply but having no idea what her words were. The distraction had overpowered his senses.

"Baileys with ice, please," she repeated. He waved another note at Jim.

"Any joy with my staff, Brian?" Jim asked.

"Yes. Thank you, Jim. Most helpful. Another Cognac for me and a Baileys."

"With ice, please," she added.

"Shall we sit over there?" he suggested, considering the need for more privacy.

They moved to a dimly lit, secluded corner of the bar.

"Well, what did you want to talk about?" she asked, leaning towards him. He looked into her eyes. He felt a warm, internal melting. Her dark brown eyes shone within a thin line of pale blue eyeliner, enhanced by well-applied mascara. Her lips were dark and silky in the light. She sat with half-open mouth, showing pure white teeth and a slight glimpse of tongue.

"Is it all right me calling you Viv outside work?" he asked, testing the water for familiarity .

"Yes. That's what my friends call me, sir." she smiled.

"Right." He fidgeted and cleared his throat, trying his hardest to retain his professional status. "I've just found out some information you won't believe," he said excitedly.

"To do with the case?"

"Yes." He related his conversation with the restaurant staff.

"Another suspect then!" she grinned, relishing the challenge.

The Cheese Murder

"Yes. We'll have to get straight onto this in the morning," he said. "You and I will go and see that Clamp character. Okay?"

"Fine with me, boss" she said, saluting. "That wasn't why you asked me here though, is it, sir?" she enquired.

"No, no. I've only just found that out. You're right. There are a few other things that I wanted to talk to you about."

He paused for a second to collect his words. He sat fidgeting and fumbling again. "The trouble is, I don't know which order to put them in. Either way, you might misconstrue what I'm..."

"Oh, Gov! Come on, just spit it out!" she laughed, seeing his discomfort. "This isn't like you at all!"

He sat back, fiddled with his fingers and sighed. "Well. You may have noticed that since Bopple left, I've been without a Sergeant?"

"Yes. I guessed you'd been working on a replacement with the Chief," she replied.

"Well, I'd like to offer you the position. You've been absolutely excellent. In fact, the only one in my team even remotely good enough." He realised his complement was somewhat back-handed and corrected himself: "What I mean, Viv, is that the rest of the guys are average or worse. But you've really stood out for me." As he spoke he glanced down at her full chest cosily slumbering under the white wool. Vivian smiled humbly.

"Yes, really stood out," he dribbled.

"Well, thank you. I don't know what to say. I'm flattered. Of course, I'd love the job."

Before she had time to progress her thanks any further, he leaned forward, lightly touching her bare fingers and looked into her round sparkling eyes.

"The other thing, Viv, is more difficult. So I'll just say it." His mouth jittered for a moment. "I. .. I think you're the horniest woman I've ever met. I can't take my eyes off you."

She looked at him blankly, motionless.

"I really do, Viv. In uniform, you're stunning. In these

The Cheese Murder

clothes you're..." he was trying to restrain himself from any crudity, "You're... you're just bloody horny. I don't know how else to put it!"

He flung himself back, arms behind his head with relief. He'd said it. That was it. It was now time to await response. He smiled a glazed smile, looking like a soppy teddy on a cheap Valentine's card.

Vivian raised her eyes and studied his silly face, calculating his likely level of sobriety.

"Are you drunk, sir?" she muttered, quizzically.

"Nope," he said, hands still behind his head, looking ultimately confident. She shuffled a bit in her chair and leaned forward again, resting her chin on one hand, twisting her hair with the other, looking straight into his eyes.

"Do you know what?" she whispered. He leant forward, mirroring her pose, staring deep into her eyes.

"What?" he whispered back.

'I've always fancied you." She smiled a kinky sort of smile, the corner of one side of her mouth rising higher than the other, her thin eyebrows lifting high, her eyelashes slowly blinking.

"Have you?" he spluttered under his breath gazing deeper and deeper into her beauty. "God..." he groaned as if every male hormone in his body was about to pop.

"The thing is, sir .. " she continued.

"Mmmmmmm?" he responded, dazed.

"This Sergeant post. Is it..."

"God no! Absolutely not!" he cried. He raced through his words, wanting to dispose of the professional formalities and return to his bursting hormones: "This is what I meant by not wanting you to misconstrue things. You'll be promoted, I assure you. It's purely coincidental that I've mentioned these two things tonight. I just couldn't wait any longer!"

" Absolutely sure, sir?" she said, still exercising caution.

"Absoutely! Hand on heart! Honest! Lord strike me down and send me to eternal damnation! Promise! Cross my heart and hope to die! Slap my face with a wet kipper..." he rambled

The Cheese Murder

deliriously.

"All right, All right!" she interrupted, laughing and grasping his hand. "I just needed to be sure."

"So what now?" he said, dropping the tempo, revisiting his sensual mood, voice husky once more.

"I don't know, sir." she said, stroking the tips of his fingers.

"Viv?"

"Yes?"

"Do me a favour."

"What's that, sir?"

"Call me Brian, please."

"Oh." Her alluring look turning to a wry grin. "Do I have to, sir?"

"Why?" he quizzed.

She giggled. "Brian was the name of a pet I had."

"A pet?"

"Yes, sir!" She started to giggle.

"A dog? Cat? Hamster?"

"No!" she shrieked uncontrollably.

"What?" he asked soulfully. She was girating with laughter, trying so hard to speak. "What? What was it?" he pleaded.

"A budgie!" She leant back on her chair, rocking feverishly. "You're a budgie!"

Fluids joined in. He couldn't help himself. The sight of this woman in such ebullient hysteria could have intoxicated a funeral procession. He tittered. Then he chuckled. Then he chortled. Then he burbled into an absolutely raucous guffaw. She continued to rock and writhe, her chair see-sawing between sturdiness and imbalance. Its back legs eventually teetered, her knees evaded the safety of the underside of the table and gravity took over. Both chair and woman swung and crunched backwards. The incident exacerbated the hysterical frenzy, Fluids rolling himself off his chair, joining her on the floor, enjoined in a turbulent scene of writhing, helpless limbs and tearful faces. He started to kiss her. She kissed him back. The

The Cheese Murder

delirium of laughing became the delirium of loving, their desires unleashed on the floor.

A pair of shoes appeared at their heads.

"Excuse me!" came the stern voice. "I hate to interrupt things but I don't think this is really appropriate, do you?"

The pair clambered up, faces soaked in tears and kisses.

"Sorry, Jim, sorry," Brian whimpered with weakness. They gathered their belongings and scurried out as if they'd been discovered behind the bike sheds. They ran into the freezing night, interlocked and giggling.

The Cheese Murder

chapter sixteen
exposed members

Brian Fluids was out of bed. He was singing buoyantly in his bathroom whilst scraping at his facial coating of shaving foam. Vivian crept in behind him, her semi-naked reflection obscured by the steam from the sink. She extended her two index fingers and prodded them playfully into his bare waist.

"Aaaagh!" he shrieked. He twisted round brandishing his razor. "Oh my God! You scared the life out of me!" he puffed.

She laughed.

"Sorry, sir! Or shall I call you Brian?!" she chuckled.

"I've cut myself, look," he said pointing to his chin, his bottom lip curling like a small child about to explode into tears. He leant down and she held his chin in her hands. "Oh, you poor little creature, let me kiss it better," she susurrated, licking and pecking his wound maternally.

"What's the time?" he asked, rinsing off the foam and rattling about with after shaves.

"Six-thirty."

"God, you better get dressed and get home to change, Viv," he advised. She agreed and tiptoed on the cold wooden floor back into the bedroom. She unbuttoned the oversized nightshirt and pulled out her arms. Fluids quietly approached and leapt on her sending her onto the bed. He wriggled around on top of her, kissing every available piece of flesh as she writhed to get free.

"Sir! Sir!" she shouted as he continued to smother her. "I've got to get home! Get off!"

He sat back apologising with a childish grin. She sat up. Both were stark naked.

"Sorry, Viv, I just can't control myself," he whispered, his large palms running down the sides of her slender back.

"Well, you'll have to learn to control yourself, won't you," she smiled, getting up and reaching for her clothes. "You'll *have* to be totally discreet at work, you know. No favouritism,

The Cheese Murder

nothing."

She walked into the bathroom clutching her bra, knickers, jumper and jeans. "If the rest of the troops even get a hint of what's going on here, " she called, "there'll be an uprising. *'She's bonked her way to promotion!'* that's what they'll say. And I wouldn't blame them."

"All right, all right! I get the message."

Eight o'clock approached and the murder team had congregated at HQ. Teeth and Crumblewick were chatting quietly and excitedly, rustling sheets of paper. Stan Stringent sat by himself clutching a video cassette to his chest. Fluids and Fledgling were whispering together. Halibut strode in, a cardboard folder under his arm, decrepit deer-stalker in hand. Fluids addressed the group.

"Right. Now you're all present, let's get some progress reports."

Crumblewick jumped up abruptly, his young, inexperienced face effervescing. "Sir, Sir!"

"Yes, Crumblewick? What have you got for us?"

Crumblewick was vibrating with ebulience. "Well, we went to see Pandora... Pandora Le Pants yesterday and it was great!" he fizzed. "Lovely paintings and loads of wine and stuff!" He continued to bounce and writhe, his legs twisting as if his bladder was set to burst. "His boots fit, they went to France that day and he's got no alibi!" The words flew out quickly and opaquely.

"Slow down, Crumblewick! Slow down! Now please clarify," ordered Fluids, calmingly.

Teeth arose, pushing Crumblewick backwards onto his chair, taking over responsibility for the information.

"What my colleague here is trying to say, Gov, is this: Pierre LePants wears size ten and eleven. He has a pair of Wellingtons which we gave to Mr Halibut for matching."

"And?" prompted the Inspector, looking to Halibut.

"The size is absolutely right, I'm convinced," Halibut

The Cheese Murder

began, his older age displaying a seniority in his mannerism. "But these boots do not match the prints. However, that does not mean to say that this man is innocent. I mean, how many people commit murder and keep the evidence in their own homes, open to discovery and incrimination?" He looked around the room, half expecting verbal acknowledgement of his reasoning.

"Thanks, Halibut. So all we know is that Pierre is not ruled out?"

"Yes, but sir!" Crumblewick piped up, waving his hand vivaciously in the air. "Sir, that's not all! The alibi: there is none!"

"Okay, Crumblewick," nodded the boss with restraint. "Does Pierre say where he was at the time?"

Teeth took over again: "Well, his wife says they went to bed early, around ten-thirty and were fast asleep before midnight but she cannot swear he was in bed at midnight. But she did say that she is easily awoken if ever Pierre gets out of bed in the night so she would have known."

"Fine. So there's no watertight alibi but if we trust Mrs LePants, her husband becomes an unlikely candidate?" questioned Fluids.

"I trust her, sir. I think she's really great! She's lovely!" bounced Crumblewick, his face still alight.

"The other thing is this, Gov," interjected Teeth. "We thought that if the killer used his own french bread and cheese, he must have bought it on the trip as well, yes?"

There were half-hearted nods from the others. "Well, we got hold of their receipt for the stuff that they bought. We have it with us and it confirms they bought nothing but wine." Crumblewick by this stage was bobbing again, flapping the receipt in his right hand, his mouth open expectantly.

"I've got the receipt, sir!" he yelled, leaning across to the Inspector. "It was my idea to get it, sir! It was my idea!"

"All right, Crumblewick. Please calm down before you have a seizure. You've done well."

The Constable returned to his chair, glowing with pride.

The Cheese Murder

"Sorry, but this receipt means nothing, does it?" challenged Halibut, peering over the Inspector's shoulder.

"How do you mean?" questioned Crumblewick, instantly deflated.

"What's to say this Pierre didn't buy the bread and cheese separately on another receipt?" quizzed the forensic king.

"Or even," Fledgling followed, "what is to say that this murder wasn't planned by two people - or even more?"

All the others looked at her, amazed at this sudden consideration.

"I cannot help thinking, you see," she continued, "that as there were at least three people with motives, this would be an ideal opportunity to collectively plan and instigate such a murder. In other words, the killer may have got the bread and cheese from someone else on the trip."

She slapped her stockinged thighs conclusively. There was an instant reactionary murmur to this observation.

"You may have a point there, Fledgling," congratulated her lover, his eyes sparkling in admiration. "We certainly need to bear that in mind, everyone."

"It is unlikely, though, that Pierre bought any bread and cheese himself, sir," continued Crumblewick defensively. "Pandora would have told us: she was with him all the time and she's a lovely, genuine lady. She wouldn't lie to us, honest!"

Fluids grunted: "You cannot judge people so simplistically. You must not trust anyone, Crumblewick."

"Pandora also mentioned the trouble on the France trip," added Teeth, "Although she's not aware of the subject of Ralph's threats, she was certainly under the impression that Pierre feared Ralph. Parmesan was aggressive towards him all day."

"Right. Thanks, lads," said Fluids. "And how have you got on, Stringent?"

Stan stood up holding his video.

"I checked Parmesan's house. There's nothing to show he bought more than three baguettes.. you know you asked me to find out..."

The Cheese Murder

"Yes, yes, Stringent. What else?"

"I went to see Leonard Mantelpiece. He seems pretty cosied up with Ribcage, you know. Anyway, I looked at his fingernails and he definitely doesn't bite them. He's got very small fingers as well, nothing like the size of those nails that Mr Halibut found. Also, sir, I checked his shoe size. Size eight, definitely."

"Well that's useful, Stan. Did Mantlepiece say anything of interest?"

"No, not really. But he seems to have an alibi: apparently he had the squits and he showed me an empty bottle of Kaolin that he'd used, you know, to stop his runny... "

"I think we get the idea!" snorted Fledgling. "Anyway, like Pierre, we've only got his word. Did he go to the doctors or anything?"

"No, he didn't. He planned to go but his arse was in such a bad state that he felt he'd have an accident in his trousers if he left his house!" grinned Stan.

The others tutted and huffed at his choice of vocabulary. "But at least his fingernails differ, sir!" he insisted.

"Anything else to add?"

"Well, I recorded the news last night for you," he smiled, waggling the cassette above him. "Can we see it, sir?"

"Okay," humoured Fluids, pointing to the TV. Stringent lunged over to the machine, inserted the tape and pressed 'play'.

"What's this?" asked Fluids, puzzled at a colourful children's animation on the screen.

"Oh, sorry! I forgot to rewind the tape," blushed Stringent. "This is an old tape I recorded The Herbs and stuff on for my son."

He fumbled with the buttons, muttering "Won't be long now... just coming up in a minute." The group sat wriggling and sighing with impatience.

"Here we go!" announced Stringent as the picture slowed to normal speed, a studio presenter introducing the story. The picture cut to the broadcast of DI Fluids outside Parmesan's

The Cheese Murder

house, surrounded by the hoards of press.

"There's me! Look!" cried Stringent, touching the screen.

"Shut up, Stringent and listen!" scolded Fluids, analysing his speech.

"Hold it, sir!" Fledgling jumped. "Stan, can you reverse it slowly and then freeze the frame?"

She stood, close to the screen. "Stop it there!" she instructed. "Look, sir," she said, pointing to the still of Stan Stringent in the background.

"What?" Fluids questioned, missing the point.

"Move it slowly on, Stan," she continued. "Now watch him," she said, her finger tracing Stringent's movements on-screen.

"What? What's wrong with me?" challenged Stringent, offended.

"You're biting your bloody nails, Constable!" retorted Fledgling. She turned towards the Inspector. "Look, sir, he's biting his damn' nails and spitting them out!"

Halibut raced to the door, barging past Teeth and Crumblewick.

"Oh come on, Vivian!" snorted Stringent, "you don't think they were *my* fingernails on Parmesan's carpet, surely?!"

"You don't even know when you're doing it, do you Stan?" she snapped.

Fluids stood silently, signalling the need for Halibut's urgent intervention. The door flung open and Halibut rushed back in carrying a tiny transparent bag.

"Over here, Constable, please" he ordered sternly. "Put your fingers on the table."

Stringent hesitated.

"Do it!" the Inspector sniped.

Halibut extracted the three pieces of fingernail shrapnel from the evidence bag using tweezers and pushed each one up to the officer's respective nails. The expert contorted his head to get a variety of views, to measure thickness and texture. The room was absolutely silent, all gathered round awaiting the forensic

The Cheese Murder

expert's judgement.

Stringent's expression was turning slowly towards one of utter humiliation.

"Well?" urged Fluids. Halibut stood back, replacing each slither into the bag.

"I'm sorry," he said.

"What? You mean they're not mine?" smirked Stan.

"No! What I mean is *they are* yours! I'm certain they're yours, *Constable!"* Halibut snapped with contempt. He looked harshly at Fluids: a look of utter disgust; a look demanding the harshest punishment.

"Halibut. Please take Stringent to your lab, get an absolute result for me and report back." Brian Fluids looked utterly outraged. The two men left the room, Stringent's head drooping in shame.

"Right, the rest of you. While that bloody mess is being cleared up, I want you to know about some new information that has come to light. We need all of your help with this. Okay?" Fluids was still aggravated.

"Yes, sir!" the three officers responded instantaneously. The Inspector related the information gleaned from Trish the waitress regarding Arbuthnot Clamp and the blackmail.

"I want you two, Teeth and Crumblewick, to get the names of all the factories around this region and find out which ones Clamp had past connections with. When you've found that out, I want you to research anything controversial that happened during that time and visit the factories, if necessary. I want to know what these threats were that Clamp was so frightened of. Understand?"

"Yes, sir!" the pair exclaimed.

"Constable Fledgling and I will go and see Clamp himself and do the necessary interrogations. Right?"

"Yes, sir!"

He motioned to them, the two men jumping up and striding out.

Brian looked at Vivian. "Well, it looks like we've found the

The Cheese Murder

fingernail culprit," he sighed, shaking his head.

"I'm sorry about that, sir, but I always thought it a bit strange that a murderer who had clearly taken such care, would leave nails lying about. Unless it was The Black Fingernail, of course!"

"God, don't apologise, Viv! He's an idiot. I'm tempted to get rid of him. He's downright incompetent and he's getting worse, not better."

"That would mean you're one short on a Constable. Does that mean my promotion..."

"Of course not, darling," he reassured, squeezing her hand. "I'll just find a replacement. No-one can be as crap as him." He stroked her cheeks and kissed her lips.

"Not here!" she whispered, pushing him away, just as Halibut and Stringent reappeared.

"What's the verdict, Halibut?" Fluids frowned.

"Guilty."

"Thank you Halibut. You can go now. Viv, can you wait outside, please?" He ushered her out, closing the door. Stan was leaning against the desk, trembling in disgrace.

"Constable Stringent," Brian began with frightening severity, waggling his fingers in front of Stan's nose. "This really is unacceptable. An officer screws up a murder scene by contaminating the evidence! You're professionalism is sadly lacking. You constantly inhibit our work. You've made the most tactless, stupid, inane comments to witnesses and victims. You show no empathy or sensitivity. In fact, Stan, you're completely bloody useless."

Fluids dropped his hands and shook his head desparingly. "I don't know what else to say."

The Constable shivered with shame, the bags under his eyes reddening and swelling. "I'm so sorry, Gov," he whimpered. His fingers raised to his mouth and he started to chew nervously.

Fluids reached out and fiercely slapped his wrist: *"Get those bloody fingers out of your mouth. Even now, after all this, you still continue to gnaw them!"*

The Cheese Murder

Stringent hastily retracted his hand and collapsed onto the desk, wailing miserably.

"Be warned, Constable, your career is in serious jeopardy over this!" yelled Fluids, storming out, leaving the man booing, blubbering and howling.

chapter seventeen
clamp and cuffs

The unmarked police car pulled up at the Sockwith Corporation Transport Bus Station. Fluids and Fledgling walked into the main office, demanding to see Mr Clamp. A scruffy little girl telephoned through to the Chief Executive's office.

"He's busy at the moment," she told the officers, chewing and slurping on some bubble gum.

"How long's he going to be?" asked Vivian.

"Dunno. Come back tomorrow some time. You can try again then, I s'pose," the girl sniffed, picking up an emery board.

Fluids leant over the girl's table authoritatively. "Look here, little girl. You telephone Clamp back and tell him that we're on our way up now. Understand?"

"Can't do that, mate, he's an important bloke. Don't care who you are." She inflated the pink gum, ballooning it into a thin, tight globe and then spattering it over her spotty chin.

"Are you going to ring him or not?" he seethed.

"Naa," she slurped, wiping away traces of the sticky gum with her sleeve and continuing to grind her nails.

"Right. Come on Constable, we'll go up anyway. Ignore this silly little girl!" They walked across the courtyard, up the stairs and along the corridor.

Fluids flung open the door. Arbuthnot Clamp was sitting at his desk, a small free-standing mirror in front of him. He was staring into it, trimming his beard with a pair of nail scissors, short black hairs falling onto a copy of Sporting Life. He looked up angrily.

"How dare you come barging in here! What gives you the bloody right?! "

"We're DI Fluids and..."

"I know who you are! We've met!" he stormed. "You still have no right to just barge in..."

"Mr Clamp, I'd advise you to calm down! We have to ask

The Cheese Murder

you some questions..."

"Make an appointment like everyone else!!" he yelled, gesturing to them.

"Mr Clamp," seethed Fluids, "you either calm down and talk to us here, or we take you down the... "

Clamp had got up. He waggled his nail scissors threateningly in front of the DI's eyes.

"Just bugger off. Go on! Just bugger off!" He pushed fiercely at Fluids and Fledgling. "Go on, get out!" he demanded.

Fluids retaliated, his strength propelling Clamp backwards, slamming him against the wall. "Constable, cuff him!" he ordered, pinning the man by his throat. Fledgling reached into her pocket, took out the handcuffs, twisted the man's torso and pulled his arms behind him, clipping them in place.

"Right, Arbuthnot Clamp: I arrest you on charges of... "

Clamp inhaled, pulled his head back against the wall and then flung it violently forward, savagely crunching Fluids' temple. Fluids crumpled to the floor. He writhed for a few minutes, touching his head for signs of blood and stumbled to his feet. He was frothing with rage.

"Right, Clamp, you've asked for it!" He twisted round behind him, wrapped his arm tightly round the man's neck and pushed.

"Move it, Clamp!" he sizzled. Fledgling grabbed his cuffed arms, pulling them high up his back. The pair heaved.

Clamp simply flopped forward onto his desk, yelling. "I'm not going anywhere, you bastards!" He writhed on the table and kicked furiously.

Fledgling drew her lapel-radio to her mouth and called for assistance.

"You're coming down the station with us, whether you like it or not. Even if it takes ten officers, get it?" Fluids foamed. Clamp turned his head and spat.

A figure appeared at the open door. "What's going on?" he asked.

"Bugger off!" yelled Clamp seeing the Accountant.

The Cheese Murder

"Give us a hand?" struggled Fluids. "We need to get this man into our car"

"Ooerr, I don't know," muttered the Accountant, fumbling.

"You help these scum and you're fired!" snarled Clamp still wrestling to get free of the officers' grips, still spread across his desk, squirming like a fish on dry land.

"Ooerr, I don't know what to do," snivelled the Accountant, taking two steps forward and two back again. "He *is* my employer, Inspector. I can't..."

"Too bloody right you can't! Now just get out!"

The Accountant continued to jig forward and backward with indecision. Police Force or Employer? Police Force or Employer? Which?

"Okay, let's make it easier for you, shall we?" said Fledgling, teeth gritted in the struggle. "Either help us with this violent man or face charges yourself for refusal to co-operate." She glanced at Fluids for approval. He nodded.

The Accountant immediately sprung into life, raced forward and grabbed Clamp by a chunk of his hair.

"Sorry, sir but I have to..." He tugged ruthlessly.

"Aaaaagh!" screeched Clamp painfully. The wrenching on his hair was acute, layers of scalp on the verge of ripping and peeling away. The Accountant towed the man across the desk, the mirror, pens, papers, ornaments and sundries propelled in the chaos, Clamps legs paddling him forward to relieve the tension on his head.

"You traitor! You bastard! You're fired!" he screamed as the trio heaved.

Into the corridor, the man barely on his feet, his legs awkwardly stumbling forward to keep up with his hair, neck and arms. They mercilessly wrenched him down the stairs, his knees crashing on the steps, Clamp yelling incessant obscenities. Two more Constables met them at the door. They lifted his legs and hoisted the struggling body into the open door of their panda car.

"Get him down the nick!" ordered the Inspector, still profoundly enraged.

The Cheese Murder

The car raced off with oscillating lights and siren. The Accountant watched, scratching and squeezing his bow-tie.

"Is he often like that?" puffed Fluids, straightening his clothing and checking his head for cracks.

"Mmm, afraid so," panted the Accountant. "He's a good businessman - but that's all."

He started to walk away.

"Hang on, sir. Can we ask you a few things while we're here?" called Fluids.

"Oh. Err, yes, I suppose you may as well, officer. Err .. come to the canteen. It'll be quiet in there for a while."

The canteen was virtually unoccupied. A couple of cooks in overalls and hats sat in the far corner smoking and drinking coffee. Clatterings of pans and plates echoed across the long room, accompanied by a faint smell of cauliflower.

"Have a seat here," the Accountant gestured. The officers sat whilst the Accountant walked over to the cooks.

"How's your head?" asked Vivian.

The man's forehead was beginning to bulge as if being blown out from the inside. The skin was stretched, purple and shiny.

"It hurts. I feel like the Elephant Man," he sniffed, secretly enjoying the attention.

The Accountant returned. "I've taken the liberty of asking them to make us some real coffee: I told them you were distinguished guests. I'm sure you'd prefer that to the vending machine?" he smiled.

"Thanks," they agreed, Fluids continuing: "We appreciate your help with Clamp just now. I realise it must have been difficult for you. Unfortunately he may be in some trouble and we really needed to get him down to the station."

"Can I ask what he's been up to? Not that Archie Pond thing again?" the Accountant asked nervously.

"Well, no. Not so much the Pond death," replied Vivian. "We're now investigating the Parmesan death."

The Cheese Murder

The Accountant looked worried. "Oh Lord," he breathed, "I feared this. I half suspected something."

"What do you mean'?" she asked.

"After I heard about Ralph I wondered about Mr Clamp."

"In what way?"

"Well, it all stems back to the Pond fiasco. As you know, Archie and Ralph were very good friends. Ralph couldn't help connecting Mr Clamp to Archie's death."

The officers nodded, fully understanding the history of this case.

"The thing is," the Accountant continued openly, "I think there was something more serious - more sinister - going on."

"Oh?"

"Yes. Last Tuesday .. No, Monday .. yes Monday around five-ish, I happened to walk in on Mr Clamp. He was in the process of half-throttling Ralph. I'd been listening at the door for a while, having heard raised voices and decided to interrupt, really just to see what was going on."

"This was in his office?" Fledgling questioned, pen back in action.

"Yes." He flapped his tie. "Anyway, he told me to get out, like he always does. I left quickly but I stood outside his door for a while longer. I know I shouldn't have but..."

"Can you tell us what the argument was about, please?" said Fluids.

"Yes. I heard a good deal of it, I think. It seems that Parmesan had arranged to meet the Sockwith Weekly with some story about Mr Clamp when he worked at Griswald's. You know, the big pie factory by the canal? Mr Clamp was denying there was anything to tell but Ralph knew better. He actually told Ralph that he was sacked but I don't think he meant it. Clamp was scared."

Vivian lifted her radio again. "Yes, Fledgling here. Can you get an urgent message to Constables Teeth and Crumblewick. Tell them that the factory is Griswald's. Yes, Griswald's. Thanks."

The Cheese Murder

"The strange thing is," continued the Accountant, "Parmesan was an ideal candidate to be given redundancy with all the new changes here, but Mr Clamp had actually completed a form for Ralph, authorising a pay rise and stating that he'd be the first of our staff to drive the new Superbus we're getting."

"Blackmail. We thought as much," commented Fluids. The Accountant nodded and opened his mouth to continue but Fluids indicated silence. One of the cooks was approaching with a tray. She placed it on the table, smiled and disappeared back into the kitchen.

"Do you know anything about Clamp and Griswalds? Anything significant?" asked the WPC, spooning sugar into Fluids' cup and stirring it for him.

"Don't you remember the scandal?" The Accountant looked surprised at their ignorance,

"No, I don't think we do," Vivian replied, halting her cup below her lips.

"There was an almighty rumpus about eighteen months ago. They called it *The Sex and Stuffing Scandal*" he blushed.

"What'?"

"Yes, *The Sex and Stuffing Scandal*. It was all to do with the Managing Director there. He was having an affair with some woman on the factory floor, a production manager, I think. She sold her story to the papers about her sordid love-life and how Griswald's were cheating on the pie fillings."

"The MD was Clamp, was it?" Fluids asked.

"Oh no. It was Mr Griswald himself. Apparently Griswald was married. This girl wanted him to leave his wife for her. But he wouldn't, so she threatened him with the press: not just about their affair but also about the way the factory had used some synthetic stuff to fill out the meat pies. He still refused to leave his wife, so she blew the lid on the whole thing."

"What happened?"

"Well, Griswald resigned and his son, Jeremy Griswald Junior took over. He promised to shake up the entire place and try to repair their reputation. Their sales really plummeted, you

The Cheese Murder

know. Their image was wrecked for a long while. It's still only now getting back to normal."

"So where do you think Clamp fits in to this scandal?" Fledgling enquired, vibrantly scribbling.

"I've no idea."

"Perhaps he was connected but never found out'?" suggested Fluids.

"Quite possibly, but I don't know. The thing is, if Mr Clamp's name ever came out, it would ruin him."

Fledgling was curious: "What was this synthetic stuff?"

"I can't remember. Something to do with seats... err, yes, soft furnishings. "

"You don't mean they used cushion and sofa stuffing in their pies?"

"Yes, that's it!" nodded the Accountant with a hint of a smirk. "A furniture factory had gone bust and Griswald's got hold of tons of the stuffing which saved them a fortune in proper pie fillings. It was found to be quite edible and very filling."

He thought further, smiled and added: "Don't you remember their slogan at the time?!" He chuckled.

"What was it?" they asked curiously. The Accountant's face creased into a fit of laughter. "Sorry, sorry," he repeated between guffaws. "I don't laugh very often, you know, but this slogan... so appropriate!" he broke into a longer fit. The police couple grinned at each other, out of pleasure at seeing this sad man transformed for a rare moment.

"What? What was the slogan?" Fledgling persisted, her expression reflecting the glow of his amusement. He sniffed, calmed down, drew a few deep breaths and said:

"The slogan was *Have a seat, have a pie, Griswald's really satisfy."*

The Accountant restrained himself for a few seconds, looking at the officers for reaction. They politely chuckled for a moment and the Accountant rocked and jerked uproariously.

Minutes passed and the Accountant gradually settled back to sobriety.

The Cheese Murder

"Is there anything else you can tell us?" Fluids asked, aware of the time and his desire to confront Clamp at the station.

"I don't think so, sir," sniffed the Accountant, drying his tearful eyes on a serviette. "Oh dear, I haven't laughed for ages. For nearly three months, to be precise."

"Oh?"

"Not one laugh. Ever since the departure of the old boss and the arrival of Mr Clamp." He carried on sniffing, his mouth falling towards a state of melancholy.

"I hate it here, sir," he muttered. "Mr Clamp is just so intolerable. He's not human." He began to snivel into the serviette. "Oh no, now I'm crying" he wailed. "Sorry, sorry!"

Fledgling got up and knelt next to him, holding his hand.

"Hey, come on, calm down. Tell us about it. Get it all off your chest," she whispered, rubbing his fingers. He sniffed a huge sniff, trembled and exhaled.

"I don't know why he has to be so nasty. He really is a nasty man. I was so happy here before he came," he blabbered, teardrops falling onto his large bow-tie, randomly dampening and darkening the large white fabric spots.

"Why is he nasty?" Fledgling asked softly, still clutching him.

"He just is. He's power-mad. If anyone crosses him, they really suffer. That's why they call him 'Castro'. He looks like him and acts like him. Completely selfish, dominating, dictatorial... no-one crosses him and gets away with it!"

"But why you? Why is he nasty to you? You seem such a harmless sort?" she questioned gently.

"Oh, I haven't done anything wrong," he snivelled, "It's just that anyone that's good at their jobs is seen by him as a threat to his power and position. He wants to keep his stronghold and so he makes everyone else feel incapable and incompetent. There's not a single person he respects..."

"And so..." Brian Fluids interrupted, calculating, "someone like Ralph Parmesan, armed with threats, who really *did* try to cross him, could well end up dead?"

The Cheese Murder

"Yes." The Accountant hesitated. "Well. Maybe."

"Well, thanks for your help," the Inspector wrapped up, standing and shaking the man's hand.

"What's going to happen?" the Accountant questioned as they turned to depart.

"How do you mean?" quizzed Fledgling.

"With Mr Clamp? What's going to happen now?"

"We'll have to see, won't we?" shrugged Fluids.

The officers left the Accountant, his solitary, morose figure silhouetted in the canteen, lonely and worried.

Back at the Police Station, Clamp was being forcibly escorted from his cell to an interview room. He was still vehemently resisting; kicking and shouting. Fluids and Fledgling paced down the corridor to meet him. Teeth and Crumblewick came out of a side door.

"Hello, Gov," said Teeth.

"How's things?" asked Fluids.

"Oh, we've had to hang around, sir. Clamp has been a real handful. He tried doing a runner twice, before we got him into the cell. He's bloody mad!"

"Mmm. Right, well, where are you off to now?"

"To see Pierre LePants, sir," smiled Crumblewick. "He's at home now with his lovely wife - you know, Pandora... I wonder if he'll offer us any wine..."

"Keep an eye on Crumblewick for me," advised Fluids to Teeth, rolling his eyes. He turned to Vivian.

"Right, let's go and meet 'Castro' shall we?"

Fledgling opened the door to the interview room, three officers restraining Clamp.

"Right," began Fluids walking up to him. "Let's have some composure. The sooner we start, the sooner you can go. Okay?"

"Give me one good reason why you've brought me here," Clamp snarled. "You and your boys have treated me like some wild animal!"

"It's your own fault, Clamp. We gave you the opportunity

The Cheese Murder

to talk in your office but you wouldn't have it, would you?"

"You're all bastards."

"If you just sit back and calm down for a minute, we'll explain why we want to talk to you."

Clamp huffed, shook off the grip of the three Constables, and leant forward, agitated but quiet.

"Thank you. Right. Now I'll explain." He signalled to the trio to move away from Clamp. "It's to do with the death of Ralph Parmesan."

"Oh, yeah? Here we go..." Clamp muttered/

"Look. All we want to do is ask you a few things so that we can eliminate you from our enquiries. That's all. Is that fair enough?" Fledgling switched on a cassette recorder and introduced those present in the room. "Right, Mr Clamp. Would you mind first telling us where you were around midnight last Tuesday?"

"Oh, right! So you think I *did* do it!" snorted Clamp, retrieving his temper.

"No we don't! We have to ask everyone. It's simply standard procedure," explained Fledgling calming her tone to reassure him.

"All right! I was out. I was entertaining a friend," he submitted.

"Can you tell us where, when and with whom, please?" continued Vivian.

"No."

"Well, it's up to you, of course. But unless we can verify your whereabouts, we can't eliminate you, can we'?"

Clamp sat quietly, fidgeting, clearly not wishing to expand.

"Fine. Well, perhaps we can return to that subject later once you're fully aware of the seriousness of this matter."

Fluids brought up the subject of Ralph, Clamp and Griswald's. The mention of the pie factory turned Clamp's complexion a ghostly grey.

"Let me make it clear, Mr Clamp," he continued, "we are *not* investigating anything to do with Griswald's. We are only

The Cheese Murder

interested in the Parmesan murder. It seems Ralph knew something, presumably to do with *The Sex and Stuffing Scandal*, that was a clear threat to your name, reputation and future career. Am I right?"

Clamp sat motionless and silent, disturbed by their level of knowledge.

Fledgling took over the questioning: "What was it, Mr Clamp? What did Ralph know that was so damaging? And is it right that he tried to blackmail you?"

"It's true he was blackmailing me," mumbled the man, his voice finally cracking with humility. "I signed off a pay rise. And I promoted him to Superbus driver..."

"Go on," encouraged the WPC.

"I don't know whether Parmesan knew anything or not about the factory. I guess he was bluffing but I just couldn't risk it."

"We understand that," comforted Fledgling. "It's a nasty business, I agree."

"The thing is, he said he'd contacted the papers with some outrageous story about me." He looked up, reviving his officious dignity. "I'm a very important man, you know. I have status in the community. I'm a valuable component in many trade and commercial institutions. If one is to maintain that level of respect and reputation, one has to do anything to avoid damage. Do you see?"

"Can I ask you outright, Mr Clamp," Fluids said, leaning forward. "Did you kill Ralph Parmesan?"

"No!" he cried, punctuating his response by bashing on the table. He looked up at them again, their expressions showing a lack of conviction. "Do you really think that someone in my position would commit the worst of all crimes?"

The officers sat quietly. Clamp was struggling to impose any level of credence.

"Look," he continued, "I don't even know how he died. He didn't turn up for work and it wasn't until around lunchtime that news came through to me that he'd been found dead."

The Cheese Murder

"Have you been to Calais recently?" asked Fledgling.

"What? No. I've never been to Calais."

"Do you know anyone that has been there in the past week or so?"

"No."

"Do you know any of the following names," she continued, "Pierre LePants..?"

"No."

"Leonard Mantlepiece?"

"No."

"Christine Ribcage?"

"Yes. His girlfriend. I met her once I think."

"Bob Rack?"

"Yes, I know of him. He works at the Minibus place."

"Reg Book?"

"No."

"Mrs or Major Bleach-Parsley?"

"No."

"What size shoes do you wear'?"

"Nine. Sometimes ten."

"Do you know any of the pubs in Larynx'? The Grinning Plank, The Blunt Raisin... or the err... "

"The Foot and Mouth?" aided Fluids.

"Yes, I know the Blunt Raisin. I occasionally eat out there."

"When were you last there?"

"Err... about three weeks ago. "

"Where were you last Tuesday night?"

"Piglings Night Club."

"Who with?"

"No comment."

"What time did you arrive and leave?"

"We got there about 9:30 and left about three in the morning."

"If you won't tell us who you were with, we'll need someone else to corroborate your story. Can you give us some

The Cheese Murder

names?"

"Of people that were there?"

"Yes."

Clamp sat back sighing. "I don't know anyone there by name. I suppose the barmaids may remember..."

"Would you accompany us to Piglings so that they can confirm this?"

Clamp sighed again. "All right, I'll tell you who I was with. But this is in confidence, right?"

"Of course," they said.

"I was with a lady called Jessica. Jessica Flummery." Clamp looked at them, expecting some sort of radical reaction. The officers looked blankly at each other.

"Jessica Flummery?" checked Fledgling. "Are we supposed to know her?"

"I'm surprised you don't. She's quite well known round here."

Fluids scratched his head. "Griswald's," he said astutely.

"Yes."

"Was she the lady involved in the pie scandal?"

"Mmm."

"Well, as we said earlier, that is of no interest to this case. Can you just tell us where we can find her, to check out your story?"

"A house called The Pines down Reservoir Lane."

"I know where you mean. Nice area," commented Vivian.

"Well, she set herself up with the money from the papers."

"Thank you, Mr Clamp. Now if all this checks out, you'll hear no more from us," she said, getting up.

"Is that it?" he said surprised

"Yes. Wasn't too bad after all, was it?" she frowned.

"No," he mumbled with regret. "I'm sorry about my behaviour. And your head, Inspector. I just panicked. I thought you may have been investigating the old Scandal. I know some day I'll be exposed for my relationship with Jessica."

"I'm just curious, Mr Clamp; why should your relationship

The Cheese Murder

be so harmful?" questioned Fluids.

"It connects me to the woman. And such a connection may lead investigations back to my part in the fiasco. I wasn't entirely innocent, you see."

"Right. Well, thanks for your honesty. I hope that you can learn to trust us in future, if ever we cross paths again."

"Are you going to press charges?" said Clamp, worried.

"On what matter?" asked Brian Fluids

"Your head. Assault on a police officer, isn't it?" he said, staring at the dark bulbous lump.

"We'll see. It depends." He ushered Clamp out of the room.

The Cheese Murder

chapter eighteen
tears, shed

Questioning continued at the LePants residence.

"Can you prove you were asleep with Pandora at midnight last Tuesday?" interrogated Constable Teeth.

"No, I cannot. How do you expect me to prove it?" the Frenchman retorted, agitated.

"Can you ride a bicycle, Pierre?" asked Crumblewick, the obscurity of his question puzzling Teeth.

"What?"

"A bicycle - you know, une bicyclette?" Crumblewick repeated.

"I know what a bicycle is! You don't have to try your dreadful French on me! Of course I can ride a bicycle!"

"Do you have one?"

"Yes."

Pandora stood up, offered the guests a coffee and left the room. Teeth leant forward, seizing the opportunity to question Pierre on the sensitive matter of Ralph's threat over revealing Christine's miscarriage to Pandora.

"How damaging do you think it would have been if Parmesan had told your wife about... you know...?" he asked quietly. Pierre was shocked that the police were so well informed.

"Please," he pleaded, "Don't ask me while Pandora is here. I don't want her knowing anything about this..."

He stood up and beckoned them through to the garden. "Darling, I'm going to talk to these policemen in the garden. Please stay in the front room, yes?"

"All right, Pierre. I'll make the coffee later." She looked worried.

The three men walked down the garden path, past the fine winter-flowering borders, under an arch of bare rose branches and past a thawing pond towards the garden shed.

The Cheese Murder

"I will be honest with you," Pierre began again, "Parmesan really frightened me. I could easily flatten him," he said, clenching his fist, "but if he ever told Pandora, I know she'd leave me. Pandora is a soft, refined lady, with high morals. And very beautiful."

"Yes, she's lovely," smirked Crumblewick. Teeth frowned at him.

"You must admit, Pierre, you did have a motive to kill him, and you can't substantiate your alibi, can you?"

Crumblewick piped up: "And you knew where he lived, you'd had a fight that day, you wear the right size boots *and* you have a bike."

"So?" questioned Pierre, arms outstretched. "Does that mean I killed him?"

"You tell us!" Teeth demanded.

"You are joking with me. Of course I didn't!" he spat.

"Is your bike in there?" asked Crumblewick pointing to the shed.

"Yes."

"Can we see it, please?"

"Why?"

"We need to check it out, if you don't mind."

Crumblewick stepped up to the shed, unbolted the door and walked inside. Garden instruments dangled neatly from hooks, several boxes piled in one corner, a shelf unit holding toolboxes and paints in another. Everything was regimentally stored away except for the bicycle which lay on the floor. The officer lifted it up and studied it closely. The tyres were caked in mud, the frame splattered with dirt.

"You'll find it clean. I always wash it after using it. I hate dirt and untidiness. I go cycling at weekends, you know," called Pierre, not even bothering to turn round.

Crumblewick climbed over the bicycle.

"Colin!" he called.

Teeth entered. "The tyre tread - looks like in the picture," he said quietly, producing a photograph commissioned by

The Cheese Murder

Halibut and distributed to each murder squad member.

"Yes, almost definitely," he agreed, carefully comparing the photo with the real tyre.

Pierre looked in. "What's going on?" he asked.

"The bicycle, Pierre. I'm afraid it matches the sort we're after. I'm sorry, Pierre, but the evidence here does seem to point to you. I have to ask you to accompany us down the station." Teeth reached out to grip his arm.

"Get off me!" he screamed, "I have nothing to do with this!"

"Come on, Pierre. We'll talk about it down the station. Please don't make things difficult for us. We're not charging you. Do you understand?"

Pierre, clearly shocked, muttering and mumbling French under his breath, walked sombrely towards the house with the police officers. Pandora came to the back door.

"Pierre? What's going on?" she asked.

"They think I did it. They think I did it!" he exclaimed, terrified.

"No, no, you've got it wrong, Constable," she said, reaching out to Crumblewick. "You can't do this to us..." she cried.

"We're not charging him, Pandora," explained Crumblewick. "I'm sorry, but he's short on alibis and I'm afraid his bicycle looks just like the one used on the night of the murder. It's exactly what we've been looking for."

Crumblewick sat in the back of the car with Pierre whilst Constable Teeth rushed back to the shed with a roll of fluorescent tape, pinning strips across the door.

"Pandora, keep away from the shed, please!" he called. "I'll be back soon to see you. Please don't worry!"

Teeth stood by his car and radio'd through to the Inspector. "Sir, I have Pierre here for further questioning. We're bringing him in. We need forensics and a van. We've found the bike. It needs collecting from their shed. Can you wait for us?"

Fluids and Fledgling waited in the police station car park

for Pierre's arrival.

Pierre spent the journey reiterating his innocence.

He was taken to the interview room and guarded whilst the officers discussed the findings.

"Did you find anything else besides the bike?" Vivian asked.

"We didn't look. We wanted to bring him in quick," replied Teeth.

"He seemed really shocked, sir," added Crumblewick. "Pierre made it quite clear that he always cleaned the bike after every trip. He couldn't believe it when we found it dirty," observed Crumblewick.

"Mmm. We'll just have to wait for Halibut, see what he makes of it."

"Could someone have borrowed it easily?" asked Fledgling.

"Well, yes," Teeth considered. "It's open access to the back garden and the shed was only secured by a simple bolt. Anyone could have wheeled the bike in and out, I suppose. That's if whoever knew he wouldn't be using it."

"Well, we'll just have to question him some more, won't we? Call me when Halibut gets back," instructed Fluids.

Leonard Mantlepiece and Christine Ribcage were spending the day transferring her personal belongings. His small red hatchback carried an assortment of furniture, clothing, plants, boxes of food and general miscellany. They had debated which items they should leave and which to take. Officially, Christine had no right to the house contents. She'd therefore been most discerning in her judgment. She assumed that Ralph's mother should be the beneficiary and therefore decided to leave the major decisions to her. She had telephoned Mrs Bleach-Parsley and arranged to meet to sort out the matter. Muriel was reluctant to get involved but appreciated Christine's dilemma. Her and the Major were due next morning (Sunday).

Lenny and Chris had thoroughly enjoyed the past few days, wrapped in the height of passion and desire. They both anticipated the return of the police, however, having only suffered the most abbreviated questioning but they had put it out of their minds. They had even forgotten to tell the police what they knew of Ralph's blackmail attempts towards Arbuthnot Clamp. They were just too busy and too happy in their own little world.

Leonard negotiated his staircase, arms supporting a tower of neatly folded clothes. Christine was in the kitchen juggling storage space for her gastronomy books and equipment, radio blaring. The front door was open, a few boxes and bags lined up in the yard and hallway ready for inspection and onward storage.

A frail voice called from the doorway. "Hello? Anyone in?!"

"Hang on!" called Leonard from upstairs. He peered down the staircase to find the small compact figure of Pandora.

"Hello, Pandora," he greeted, descending the stairs clutching a couple of white bras. "How are you?"

"Dreadful, Leonard. I need to talk."

He approached her, noticing her tear-drenched cheeks and blotched eyeliner.

"Come in to the front room." He guided her in. "Sorry about the mess. We're just moving Chris's stuff in."

He slid a few suitcases away from the sofa and lifted a large cheeseplant that was sitting precariously on the arm.

"Please, sit down, Pandora. Do you want a drink? Whisky? Gin? Rum?" he offered, opening a scruffy teak cupboard and displaying a huge range of spirits while stuffing the bras into his trouser pocket.

"Bacardi, please, Len. Thanks." He pulled out an almost full bottle, unscrewed the cap and scuttled into the kitchen.

"Chris, Pandora's here. She looks awful," he closely whispered under the radio din. He reached up for some glasses. "Do you want one?" he asked, showing her the bottle.

The Cheese Murder

"Yes, okay," she smiled, walking into the front room. "Hi, Pandora, what's the matter?"

Pandora was quietly sobbing into a tiny frilly hanky.

"It's my Pierre. The police have taken him away," she snivelled. Leonard turned off the radio and returned with three tumblers of neat Bacardi.

"Do you want any Coke or...?"

They both nodded and he filled their glasses to the brim.

"Here, knock this back, Pandora." He knelt on the floor next to the seated women.

"Apparently the police have taken Pierre," explained Chris while Pandora gulped at her white rum.

"Whatever for?" said Lenny in surprise.

Pandora looked at him, wiping her eyes, smudging the dark make-up horizontally. "They think he killed him," she sobbed.

"Who? Ralph?"

"Yes," she dribbled. "I don't know what to do, I didn't know who to talk to... " She buried her dainty round head into her dainty round handkerchief, daintily weeping.

"I can't believe this!" exclaimed Leonard. "How on earth can they think he did it? He wouldn't, would he?!" He looked at Christine, sitting silently serious. He frowned at her questioningly. She subtley patted her tummy, reminding Leonard of the miscarriage. Leonard shook his head dismissively.

"What reason did they give for taking him off?" he asked.

She explained between intermittent sobs about the mystery threat from Parmesan, the lack of alibi and the bicycle removed from the shed. "The thing is," she continued, "I *know* him. I *know* he wouldn't do this! He may be hot-tempered but *never* this! If only I knew what his rows with Ralph were about. I might be able to understand the whole thing a bit better!" she declared, her handkerchief already saturated.

"Got a hanky, Len?" asked Chris. Leonard reached into his pocket and pulled out a bra. He grinned stupidly, handing it to his girlfriend. She stuffed it down the back of the settee in embarrassment.

The Cheese Murder

"Do you really want to know what they were rowing about, Pandora?" Chris asked quietly. "Its not nice, I'm afraid. I didn't want you ever to know about it."

"I have to know! If you know, you *must* tell me. Please!" she pleaded. Leonard nodded at Chris.

"Go on, tell her. She does have a right to know. Particularly with Pierre in trouble."

Christine slowly and ashamedly recounted the story: Pierre's past violence, the miscarriage and his deepest, sincerest regret ever since.

"I told Ralph about it one night - I can't even remember why - but I never ever imagined that it would result in this! Please believe me, Pandora," she begged apologetically. "It was confidential. Pierre repented from the day I walked out on him and it's taken him all this time to be accepted back into the village and settle down with you. You have to put it out your mind. It's history. It mustn't affect your relationship with Pierre. You're so good for each other!"

"Pierre was obviously worried about this getting back to you, otherwise he wouldn't have stood for Ralph's behaviour," Len explained.

Pandora was in mild shock. She shook her head. "I don't know what to think," she muttered, staring into space. "I knew he used to be violent but that's awful. I'm so sorry for you, Chris. But he has changed. We love each other. I wish he had told me. I would have trusted him."

"Well, surely that's good then?" replied Chris, smiling and patting her shoulder. "He must have been terrified that he'd lose you if you found out."

"No... I would have stayed with him. I love him," she sniffed. "But the thing is, the police must think this is why he killed Ralph. To stop him ever telling me."

"Yes," nodded Leonard. "It looks that way, doesn't it?"

"But if he did kill him, God forbid, he wouldn't have been able to hide it from me. He would have behaved strangely, surely? You can't kill someone and then just carry on normally?"

The Cheese Murder

Pandora reasoned. "And why on earth would he have left the bicycle in that state? He is obsessed with cleanliness."

"It doesn't seem to make sense, does it?" concurred Chris, looking at Leonard.

"I don't know," he replied. "I don't know how these things work, I'm afraid." He stood up and reached for their glasses. "Another drink?" he asked.

"Well, Halibut? What's the verdict?" asked Fluids, peering at the bicycle inverted on a stainless steel table in the Path Lab like an animal's carcass.

"Definitely the bike," nodded Halibut.

"Yes, we've studied this body closely, closely," added Writhingoose, momentarily forgetting the subject. "Distinct lack of blood though, he grinned, his eyes crinkled behind his fat glasses.

"Mmm. Funny," mumbled Halibut, humming loudly.

"You're absolutely sure?"

"Mmm. It's as I thought," continued Halibut. "The pattern from the tread is identical, look," he said, lifting a large piece of paper from the floor, printed with the bicycle's tyre marks. He placed it on the table. Fledgling bent down to study it alongside the photograph.

"I agree," she said. Her hand slipped on the sheet of paper causing it to waft back onto the floor, landing wrong-side up, displaying a glossy colour poster of a tanned topless girl in a floral straw hat and grass skirt.

"Oh," coughed Writhingoose. "I err... I couldn't find any other paper," he spluttered, picking it up and having a quick close look. "I found it lying around in my locker... I mean, in someone's locker..."

"Well, never mind that," said the Detective Inspector sternly. "Let's get back to the matter in hand, shall we?"

"Right. Let's get on then," agreed Halibut. "I've taken samples from the tyre and there's an old leaf here which could

The Cheese Murder

well have come from Parmesan's apple tree."

"Are there any fingerprints or anything else on the bike of interest?" enquired Vivian.

"No. Nothing." said Halibut.

"What do we do now then?" asked Vivian Fledgling.

"We really need to find the other evidence, don't we?" said Fluids. "The Wellingtons, the gloves - even the bread and cheese that Halibut here was convinced had been removed from the scene."

"What's the French chap said?" asked Halibut as he lifted the bicycle from the table.

"He's denying everything..." Fluids paused and reached out to grab the saddle as Halibut lost his grip, the bicycle frame twisting, landing on Halibut's shoulders, the oily chain grazing his bald head. "All right, Halibut?" he said removing it carefully.

"Mmm. Yes. I'll get on then." He rubbed his black serrated scalp and hummed his way out of the room.

"I'll keep this as supporting evidence, evidence," said Writhingoose pointing to the girlie pin-up.

The Cheese Murder

chapter nineteen
kids and a nose

"I haven't the foggiest idea what to do with all this, have you Major?" said Muriel distastefully surveying the contents of the lounge at number 10 Church Lane. "None of this is remotely suitable for our house, is it? It lacks a certain quality."

"Perhaps we could donate it to some deserving charity, dear?"

"Oh, I can't be bothered with all that!" she buffed.

"Or Mrs Chaffinch? She's going to have to retire soon and she'll need accommodation of her own. Perhaps she'd be grateful for... "

"Certainly not! I'm not helping *her,* the doddery old goat!" She turned to Christine: "Is there anything here that *you* particularly want?"

"Well, some, I suppose. As you know, I'm living with Lenny now, but I guess we could use some of it. What do you think, Len?"

"Well, yes. But the Major's right. There are much more deserving causes: it's not as if we're short of money."

"Look," interrupted the Major. "It's a week until Christmas. There must be local charities that would be delighted to take some of this off your hands, to give to those less fortunate."

"Yes, I agree," Chris continued, "It's Christmas. Let's do our bit, something worthwhile. A charity or two! Yes!"

"Well, if that's what you want," Muriel sneered. "Personally I think people should make their own fortune. I have no sympathy for that sort, the penniless outcasts. But if it makes you feel better..."

"Right. That's settled then," clapped the Major. "If I were you, Chris, I'd take anything you want and then call a few charities and get them to take the rest away."

"Fine. But only if that's all right with you, Mrs Bleach-Parsley. This is all yours, after all, isn't it?"

The Cheese Murder

Muriel nodded, "Yes, yes yes, go ahead. But don't tell them it's from me. It would ruin my reputation."

"Right."

"Shall we go then?" She tugged on the Major's jacket.

"What about these? Would you like to take these?" asked Christine, handing a small stack of cards to her. "They're some old Christmas cards and photos of Ralph. I thought you might like them."

Muriel flicked through them. "These are his personal Christmas cards, are they? Two? My word, he was more popular than I imagined, " she snorted sarcastically. "And these photos ... they're of him are they? No, I don't think so." She shoved them back at Christine. The Major surreptitiously took them from Chris, sliding them into his inside pocket and winking.

"Come on, let's go. Jilks will be getting restless," Muriel ordered. "Goodbye."

"What a strange woman!" grinned Leonard as they disappeared.

The couple set to work labelling items to keep and those for donation. The front door clattered and a uniformed man peered through the leaded window.

"Hello, officers," said Leonard, opening the door.

"Sorry to disturb you both. We need to check a couple more things with you," said Teeth.

Teeth and Crumblewick stepped in and greeted Christine.

"Please, sit down," she gestured. "I would offer you a drink but we've cleared it all out."

"Oh," said Crumblewick disappointed. "What are you doing then?"

"Well, we're deciding what to keep for ourselves, you know, to move to Leonard's, and what to donate to charity for Christmas."

"Oh that's a nice gesture," complemented Crumblewick. "So you're officially back together?"

"Yep!" replied Lenny proudly. "And we're going to get married. We're going to keep Christine's original wedding

The Cheese Murder

arrangements!"

"Ahh. Congratulations!" gleamed Crumblewick. "I'm glad you're sorting yourself out, Miss Ribcage. Can I have an invitation to your wedding?"

Teeth tutted.

"Just a few more weeks and she'll be Mrs Mantlepiece!" beamed Len, squeezing her waist.

"Well, do carry on with what you're doing," said Teeth. "If we could just fire some last minute things your way?"

"What's happening to Pierre?" asked Chris, scratching her head whilst making a decision about whether to keep the coffee table.

"Give it away," indicated Leonard.

She stuck an adhesive label onto the surface.

"Pierre's still at the station. We had to keep him overnight. It doesn't look too good for him, I'm afraid. But there are a couple of things that we need to clear up that don't quite make sense."

"Oh? What?" asked Leonard.

"Well," continued Teeth, "the trouble is, although the evidence does point to him, we're still missing some vital pieces of the jigsaw."

"Has he confessed then?" said Chris, shocked at the progress report.

"No, he hasn't. In fact he continues to deny the entire thing. That's the problem: anyone can make denials. So it's down to supporting evidence."

"I went to see Pandora earlier," stated Crumblewick. "She's in a really bad way. I really feel for her," he admitted affectionately.

"Yes, we saw her yesterday," replied Chris, busying herself once more, labelling a row of books and ornaments.

"That china vase..." pointed Crumblewick. Chris looked round at him. "Yes," he nodded, "that old cream floral one with the dead freesias.".

"What about it?" questioned the puzzled girl.

The Cheese Murder

"Could I... " he cleared his throat, embarrassed.

"You want it, Constable?" she laughed.

He nodded boyishly. "If that's okay... I mean... "

"Of course you can. Here." She passed it to him.

"My wife will love this," he smiled. "She collects these sort of things."

He placed it on the floor. "Thank you. "

"Anything else you'd like?" she mused.

"No!" said Teeth sharply, glaring at his colleague. "Now," he continued formally, "Mr Mantlepiece, we need to clarify a few things about Monday and Tuesday. You say you were ill?"

"That's right."

"And you called your boss on Monday morning?"

"That's it," he said nonchalantly, raising a table lamp and signalling to Chris that he wanted it. "Yes. I rang him early so I could get down the doctors for half-eight nine-O'clock."

"But you didn't go?"

"No." He looked up at them. "My bowels were not good."

"We understand from talking to the girl in the café that Christine here tried to ring you and knocked on your door a few times during the day. Can you explain why you didn't answer?"

"Yeah. I'd unplugged the phone. The phone's downstairs and I didn't want to get up more than I had to."

"And what about the door?"

"I must have been asleep. The bug really took it out of me."

"So you were in all day Monday and Tuesday?"

"Yes."

"He must have been in, officer," interrupted Christine. "His car was outside each time I went round there. What does it matter, anyway?"

"Probably doesn't," he admitted. "I just wanted to be clear, that's all."

"You had a motive though, didn't you?" said Crumblewick, the direct poignancy of the question shocking the couple.

"No, I did *not* have a motive!" he announced. "Just because

The Cheese Murder

I love Chris and she was with Ralph... I'd waited a year and would have waited another year if necessary to get her back!" The pair clutched each other, united.

"It's true!" Chris emphasised. "His patience, devotion and loyalty would have won me back in the end."

"Anyway," continued Leonard sharply. "Your Constable friend, Stringent, he's asked me all this!"

"Yes, we realise that," admitted Teeth. "But we need to re-check. Stringent can be a bit..."

"A bit of a pratt?" nodded Lenny. "Anyway, Stringent did say that you were only investigating people who went on the trip to France. That's right, isn't it'?"

"Yes, it seems that way," confirmed Crumblewick,

"Well you know I didn't go, don't you'? Ask Bob, if you want. He'll confirm I didn't go!"

"We already know you didn't go, Mr Mantlepiece."

"Did anyone bring you back anything from France?" asked Crumblewick, hoping to hear the words 'bread' and cheese' in his reply.

"Yes. Both Bob and Christine."

"What did they get you'?"

"Fags. Two hundred B&H from each of them."

"Oh," responded the disappointed Crumblewick. "Nothing else? No food?"

"No."

"Bob and I bought the cigarettes at the same time," said Christine. "I'm a bit concerned by your questions," she continued. "You don't suspect my Len, surely?"

"Well maybe you're both in it together?" uttered Crumblewick.

"Oh, don't be stupid!" cried Christine. "We had no reason! Ralph and I had already agreed to split up. I had no motive, I've already explained."

"Have you told them about Ralph blackmailing his boss yet, Chris?" asked Leonard. "They ought to know..."

"You knew about that, did you?" interjected Teeth.

The Cheese Murder

"Yes," said Christine. "Sorry, we've been a bit sidetracked..."

"When did you know exactly?" quizzed Teeth.

"Well, Ralph told me. I just hadn't got round to telling you."

"Miss Ribcage! You could have saved us a lot of time and trouble if we'd known straight away! This really is very serious. And how long have you known, Mr Mantelpiece?"

"Oh, only a day or two," replied Leonard vaguely, realising the severity of withholding such valuable information.

"This is not good for either of you," said Crumblewick. "We're going to have to..."

A message suddenly spurted through on Constable Teeth's radio. Teeth dragged it to his mouth. "Right. We're on our way!"

"We'll have to leave it there." said Teeth putting on his helmet. "We'll have to come back and continue this discussion. You're going to have to tell us everything."

"Must dash," said Crumblewick, picking up his vase of dead freesias and hurrying after his colleague.

The police car zoomed through Larynx and along the Sockwith Road. It screeched left at a countryside junction, rocked down a half-made road and halted by a jetty a few inches from the canal. A few barges lay redundant along the bank, swans drifting around in search of food. The DI's car was parked on a soft grassy bank.

"Ah, there you are!" called Fledgling. "Come over here!" She gestured to the two Constables as they squelched their way along the towpath to the group of people, huddled together alongside a third barge moored round a bend in the river.

"What have you got, sir?" asked Crumblewick. Two frogmen were removing their flippers and masks and a young couple in bright yellow anoraks stood silent and dazed.

"See to these two people, Crumblewick. Get a statement," Inspector Fluids ordered, guiding two teenagers towards him.

"Eh?"

The Cheese Murder

"Interview them, Crumblewick!"

"Right, sir." He led the young couple, a girl and a boy, back to his car. "Sit in here, it's a lot warmer," he said, opening the rear door. They clambered in. "I'll get in with you. Shift up," he smiled, pushing them. He contorted his body onto the back seat causing great discomfort all round. "Perhaps this wasn't a good idea," he muttered, heaving himself out again, climbing into the front, twisting round and kneeling on the driver's seat, his head bent at an angle against the roof lining. He rummaged for his notebook, resting it on the headrest just beneath his chin. The young pair just sat.

"Right. What can you tell me then?" he said, pen poised. They just sat, their expressions nondescript.

"Come on!" he encouraged. "What's happened?"

The boy, around fourteen, looked up at him, his freckled face encloaked in the yellow plastic hood.

"We saw this thing in the water," he squeaked.

"Oh? What sort of thing?" Crumblewick asked.

"This big, bloated thing," the squeaky boy continued.

"What big bloated thing?"

"Big and bloated, it was. "

"What was it, sonny boy?" he pursued.

"This black, shiny thing. Next to the boat thing."

"A black shiny thing," repeated Crumblewick, baffled.

"Was it a large fish?" he guessed. The boy shook his head.

"Was it a dinghy?" The boy shook his head.

"Was it Nessie?" The boy shook his head again.

"Oh, come on, lad. Please help me out! This is worse than Give Us A Clue!"

"It had legs."

"Right," puffed the officer, still confounded. "So it was big, black, shiny and had legs." He attempted to scribble the words in his notebook in the confined space, the end of the pen poking into his cheek.

"So what was it?"

The boy just stared.

The Cheese Murder

Crumblewick puffed again.

"Big, black, shiny with legs..?" he repeated. "Was it a dining table?"

The boy shook his head.

"A wardrobe?"

The boy shook his head.

"A big wet dog?"

The boy shook his head.

Crumblewick sighed noisily. "A horse? A cow? A pig?" He sighed even louder. "Bloody hell, boy! Was it a... a... donkey? An elephant? A frigging bison? What? I give up!"

He stared at him, then her. The girl just gazed out of the window, seemingly remote from the interrogation. *"Please!* Can *you* help me, lovey?" he pleaded, stretching his neck to face her. "Please, dear. Another tiny clue perhaps?" She opened her mouth.

"Yes? Yes?" he urged. She shut it again. Crumblewick twisted round and sat facing the windscreen mumbling. He looked into the mirror at the brainless pair.

"I'll tell you what," he huffed in resignation, "I'll just sit here. And when you feel ready to talk, just let me know. Take your time. There's no rush. Just take it easy. Have a sleep if you want. Don't feel obliged to speak," he ranted sarcastically, sprawling exhausted across the steering wheel.

"A bod..." squeaked the boy.

"A what?" trilled the Constable twisting back round, catching his trouser leg on the gear stick. *"Say it again, boy! Say it again!"* he pleaded, wrestling with his leg.

"A bod..." he squeaked again.

"A bod? What's a bod?" Crumblewick cried. *"What in God's name is 'a bod', sonny??"*

"A bod... eeee"

"Oh! *You mean a body! You mean a body... as in dead body, Yes?"*

The boy nodded quietly in his hood.

"A man's body?" continued Crumblewick.

The Cheese Murder

"No" said the boy.

"A woman's?"

"No."

" A child's?"

"No."

"A dog's?"

"No."

"A horse's?" Crumblewick's face was reddening by the second.

"No."

"Oh, for heaven's sake! What sort of body was it? I can't cope with this! Please try a bit harder!" he yelped, again turning to the girl praying for some sensible enlightenment. She just looked out the window.

"So. You saw a body, yes? But it wasn't a person or a dog or a horse...?"

"No."

"Christ! Do you want me to go through every large black creature in the animal kingdom? Would that help?" he said gritting his teeth, his eyes and cheeks burning red with frustrated anguish. The girl moved her head. Crumblewick's head jerked quickly in anticipation.

"Yes? Yes? Please... say something! Go, on! Something useful! Try! Try! Pleeeeease!" he warbled, bouncing energetically on his seat, the entire vehicle rocking and swaying.

"It wasn't a body," she said, her voice in ultra-high frequency.

"It wasn't a body? Aaaagh!" wheezed Crumblewick, pulling at his hair. "Well. We thought it was," she shrilled, "But it wasn't."

"What was it then? What was it then?"

"Some stuff," the boy squeaked. Crumblewick wriggled his fingers in his ears, aggravated by the mix of senseless, dissonant, piercing vocal noises.

"Fine. Thank you. You've been so bloody helpful. Please don't bother any further," he panted, flopping back on his seat.

The Cheese Murder

"Just give me your names and I'll let you go."

"I'm Darren."

"Darren. Darren what?"

"Darren Dunkley."

" And I'm Petra. "

"Do you have a surname?"

"Yeah."

"Well what is it?" he hissed.

"Crispit."

"Right Thank you, you can go. Go on! Go!" he seethed, flapping his notebook.

The yellow anoraks speedily creaked out of the car. The officer sat for a moment, half-destroyed by the experience. "Come on Crumblewick! You love this job!" he said to himself, slapping his cheeks. He took a deep, deep breath, pulled himself out of the panda car and strolled towards the other officers, still shaking his head and muttering.

Halibut was on all fours, the silvery gaffer tape on his deer stalker dazzling in the lunchtime sunshine. He was humming loudly whilst he inspected the contents of the bundle retrieved from the canal. Fluids, Fledgling and Teeth stood around him chattering. The frogmen had gone.

"Hello, sir," said Crumblewick. "What is all this stuff, then?"

"Take a look, Crumblewick," offered the Inspector, stepping aside. "What do you make of it?"

The young Constable bent down over Halibut and perused the various items lined up on a large sheet. "Good Lord! It's the missing pieces from the murder scene!" he exclaimed excited.

"Yes. But not all of them," replied Fluids, pointing. "We've got the bread, the cheese, the wellies, the black bin liner with a hole, the coat-hanger wire..."

"Wire?"

"Yes. Remember? The killer used some wire to poke out the back door key and slide it under the door? And the bin liner was used to drape around Parmesan's head?"

The Cheese Murder

"Oh yes!"

"And," continued Fluids, "two polythene bags. "

"What were they for?" asked Crumblewick.

Halibut explained, still looking down, fiddling with tweezers and magnifiers.

"These bags were used to line the boots to make sure the killer didn't leave any skin or hairs inside the boots. And he wore thick socks too - there are several woollen fibres."

"Where are the socks?" Crumblewick enquired.

"Not here. No socks, no gloves," confirmed Halibut between further spates of humming.

"Presumably *they* would have given us the most information, the socks and gloves, with skin and prints and stuff?" assumed Crumblewick.

"Correct, Constable. Well done!" congratulated the Inspector.

"The two brain dead youngsters I interviewed for you, sir..." continued Crumblewick, "They said they thought it was a body. Big, black and shiny with legs. What made them think that..?"

"All of these items were in two carrier bags tightly sealed. The bags were then wrapped with string in some black overalls which we suspect were worn for the murder."

"Oh?"

"Yes, over there." Fluids pointed behind Vivian to a separate pile.

"The bags were so tightly sealed that they acted like balloons or buoys, causing the whole thing to float. It must have travelled a good few miles down the canal before getting tangled on the side of the barge. So it did look a bit like a drowned body, I suppose."

"The killer slipped up there, then, forgetting the thing would float and eventually be found!" commented Teeth.

"Not really," mumbled Halibut, still engrossed. "There's little here of any use. It confirms all our thoughts on how the murder was carried out but gives us no further clues to the

The Cheese Murder

killer's identity."

"But surely the boots verify the man's feet size?" queried Teeth.

"Sadly not," said Halibut, slowly getting up. "All we know is that he has size ten feet or less. "

"Eh?"

"How big are your feet, Constable Teeth?" asked Halibut illustrating the point.

"Eight."

"Well, you could have worn these boots then, couldn't you, particularly with thick socks?"

"Oh, I see!" he smiled, enlightened.

"And, in case you're wondering," continued Halibut, "the overalls tell us nothing either. The same thing applies: they're pretty large, so again, virtually anyone could have worn them. And sadly the canal water has dispersed any possible evidence that may have been lurking."

"Right, everyone, if you could bag-up everything individually and put them in the boot of my car, please," instructed Fluids. "Then we can all get off, okay?"

Halibut and Fluids walked to their cars talking, leaving the three Constables. Fledgling picked up the overalls and string, inserting them into a large clear bag. She carried it to the car. Colin Teeth did the same with the boots and Crumblewick followed behind with the wire and bags.

Fledgling proceeded back to the remaining items. Two swans had climbed up onto the bank and discovered the stale french bread lying unguarded on the plastic sheet. Their long necks slowly descended.

"Oh shit!! They're going for the bloody bread!" Fledgling yelled, running towards the birds. The other officers looked round. All but Crumblewick raced over to help.

"Get away! Shoo! Get lost! Bugger off!" they all shouted, hurling their arms in the air and dancing round the swans in a bid to scare them off. The yellow bills hurriedly snapped at the bread, pulling at it and engorging half each. They spread their

The Cheese Murder

mighty wings and flapped aggressively. Crumblewick stood back from the scene witnessing five grown people and two birds engrossed in a frantic fandango, all hurling abusive noises. The swans joined in, honking crazily.

"Retreat and they'll calm down!" shouted Fledgling above the din. "Retreat, retreat!"

The officers all stepped backwards enlarging the circle around the birds. One leapt straight into the water. The other decided to perpetuate the game. Its evil little eyes picked out Constable Teeth, fixed a demonic stare, stretched out its lengthy roll of feathery neck and thrust its head towards him. It snapped and snapped and snapped, the Constable stepping back, back and further back, yelling tortuously. Then the beast pounced, lunging high, wings and neck outstretched and plucked at the man's face. Its beak fastened upon the Constable's nose and wrenched, yanking the man forward, pulling, wriggling and twisting its head, the officer slipping and slithering in the mud, beak still attached. The swan finally released him from its grip and flapped away, leaving Teeth squirming in the mud clutching his torn, blooded nose, groaning in agony.

"Quick, get him in the panda car!" screamed Fluids. "Stick the siren on, Vivian! Get him to hospital! Go like the clappers! *Go! Go! Go!*"

Crumblewick and Halibut lifted the howling man and rushed him to the car, throwing him onto the back seat. Vivian had the engine running, the wheels spun and the car roared backwards, disappearing up the hill in reverse, the siren submerging the victim's frenzied squeals.

The Cheese Murder

chapter twenty
passion and desire

It was Monday morning, the week before Christmas. Sockwith General Hospital was playing host to the injured Constable Teeth. He lay in bed, a wide bandage wrapped tightly around the middle of his face, supporting further layers mounted on the remains of his nose. His eyes poked out from the top, watching as the door opened. Fledgling and Fluids entered, both in casual dress.

"We've brought you these," said Vivian, handing him a large, brilliant bouquet of flowers. "How are you, Colin?"

"Ugg," he replied, swallowing and wheezing through his dried mouth.

"Did you manage to sleep all right?" asked Brian, wandering around the private room.

"Ugg."

"Nice room," said the Inspector. "Your own telly. Nice."

"Ugg."

"Have they managed to fix your nose?" asked Vivian, sitting on the bed. Teeth shook his head, slurping to lubricate his mouth.

"No," he croaked. "I've got to stay in for plastic surgery."

"God, that's awful. We're so sorry it happened, aren't we sir?"

"What? Oh, yes! A dreadful thing," replied Brian Fluids, pacing round the room.

"Shame Crumblewick didn't help. He just stood there watching," Teeth said hoarsely.

"He had a similar ordeal, he tells me. He's been scared stiff of swans ever since," said Fluids.

"Oh?"

"When he was five. He was with his mum and he had to relieve himself by a river, apparently."

"Ouch!" hissed Teeth, picturing the scene.

The Cheese Murder

"Yes. Nasty business. They're so vicious, those bloody creatures."

"He's got a boy, Crumblewick, hasn't he?" said Teeth.

"Yeah .... Oh, no .. he just needed a sort of circumcision apparently. The swan just nicked his skin but..."

"Oh."

"You'll be all right, Colin," soothed Fledgling, clutching the arm of his stripy pyjamas. "It's amazing what they can do these days with plastic surgery."

"Yeah, I can imagine. Spending the rest of my life walking round with a bit of my bum glued to my face," he mumbled sadly. "What's going on now with the investigation, sir?"

"Don't know, really," he admitted. "I'm stuck. We've had to release LePants. It's sort of stalemate."

He looked out of the window, studying the view of muddled buildings below. "I just need some inspiration... or one more piece of info from somewhere," he said, clenching his fist. "Any thoughts, you two? Anything?"

"Don't know, sir," replied Teeth, his tongue wetting his mouth further and beginning to dribble.

"Clamp's clean," Fluids continued, "On this investigation, anyway. His alibi checks out. It must be Pierre."

"What about Leonard and what's-her-name?" said Teeth, rubbing away the dribbles with his sleeve.

"Christine? Why do you say that?" said Fledgling, passing him a tissue.

"Something's not right. Did Crumblewick tell you that they both knew about Ralph blackmailing Clamp but didn't bother telling us? And they're just too smug."

"They knew all along? Why on earth didn't they tell us?"

"They reckon they'd just forgotten, distracted by setting up home together."

"Mmm. Yes, I agree. It doesn't sound right at all."

Colin Teeth gently prized the bandage from his face to let in some cool air. "The thing is, Mantlepiece doesn't really have an alibi. He basically vanished for two days. He seems harmless

The Cheese Murder

enough but we shouldn't ignore that fact..."

The door opened and Crumblewick poked his head round.

"Am I interrupting or...?" he whispered.

"No, come in, Constable," said Fluids. "Colin here is just pointing out that Leonard and Christine knew about the blackmail all along, and he doesn't really have an alibi."

"But he didn't go to France," observed Crumblewick, passing a bag of fruit to the invalid.

"Thanks, Craig," said Teeth, passing the bag to Vivian, who stood and emptied the fruit into a bowl.

"I'll tell you what, Colin," reassured Fluids, "I'll go and see him. You never know, you might be right. We need to investigate further. Coming, Viv?"

"Yes," she said. "I'll pop in later, Colin." She smiled and patted his shoulder.

The Inspector and Constable began their journey to Larynx to question Leonard once more. "You ought to change into uniform, Viv. You look a bit too casual and far too sexy. Shall we stop at your place? Just up here isn't it?"

"Yes. Next left, then left again." The car entered a small, modern estate of yellow brick houses, some large, detached and executive, others further into the estate, small and boxy. Vivian walked up to the door of her small boxy one.

"Wait for me!" called Brian, running up to join her.

"I'm only going to get changed, sir!"

"Only?!!" he puffed.

"Oh, come on in then," she tutted, smiling. The front door opened and they walked directly into her lounge, a long narrow tidy room with open stairs rising up one wall. "I'll put the kettle on," she said, sliding back a glass door to the kitchen. "Coffee?"

"Yes, please," he called. "You've got a message on your machine."

"Oh. Have I? Can you play it for me, please?" she replied whilst spooning a teaspoon of ground granules into each mug. Fluids pressed 'play'.

The Cheese Murder

"Hello .. err it's John here at United Travel. Can you ring me, please. It's about your holiday. I'm afraid we're going to have to change the dates. Can you call me, please. Thanks. Bye. Oh, err, it's John - I might have said that already but in case I didn't, I have now .. err, yes, bye. Bye." The answer-machine beeped and clicked.

"Holiday? When are you going on holiday, Viv?"

"Oh, not until February. I fancied a break away in the Canaries. I need a bit of sun. It seems they've screwed up my booking, doesn't it?" she said quietly, Fluids leaning on the kitchen door frame whilst she poured and stirred.

"By yourself?" he enquired.

"Umm. No. I've booked for two."

"Oh?" Brian looked agitated. "May I ask who the other..."

"You may," she teased, passing him a mug.

"Is it a man?"

"Mmm."

"Oh? Who?"

"That would be telling, wouldn't it?" she said, passing him a mug.

"Viv. Don't be like that. If you're going with another man, I think you should tell me." He looked deeply hurt. "I know I'm old and crusty. I knew it wouldn't be long before you found some young hunk..."

"Don't be daft, " she said, pressing her body against his. "It's you. I thought we could go away together for a long weekend, relax a little and things..."

"Things?"

"Yes. You know..." she said, wiggling gently against his torso.

"Oh God..." he panted. "Let me put this coffee down, Viv."

"Certainly not, sir! We're on duty. No time for hanky panky. Wait there while I go and change."

She trotted up the stairs into the tiny square bedroom. Fluids stood debating whether to pursue his pelvic desires. He grinned, put his coffee down, removed his shoes and crept

The Cheese Murder

slowly and stealthily up the wooden stairs, crawling onto the landing and peeping into her bedroom. Vivian, in just bra and knickers, was pinning up her hair in preparation for her police hat.

Brian sighed and crawled quietly forward into the room. She turned towards him, looking upwards, and lifted her uniform which was dangling on a coathanger from the picture rail. Brian had ducked behind the bed, poking his face round the side, looking up at her pale thighs and skimpy white silk undies.

As she turned away, he bounced up, preparing to hurl himself at her. His head bashed flatly on a pine shelf above him, the shelf immediately dismantling itself from the wall. The wooden plank and twenty bottles of perfume instantly tumbled, battering and pelting him. He protected his head with his hands and curled up on the floor as if faced with a live grenade. "Shit! Ahh! Oooh!" he yelped as he was bombarded with the heavy objects. Vivian came over, laughing. "Serves you right, you pervert!" she chortled.

"Help me, Viv, I'm wounded!" he whimpered. She ignored him and dressed quickly, still laughing. Fluids climbed up onto the bed, moaning. "I am hurt, Viv, really I am!"

"Where?" she said.

"All over. Look at my head... I think its broken. It's only just recovered from Clamp's headbutting..." he whined.

She leant over him. He grabbed her round the waist and heaved her on top. "God, I love you, you sex-mad beastie!" he flubbered, his hands commencing their ritual grope.

"Not now! Please!" she struggled. "Control yourself!"

"But I have to control myself all day at work. I can hardly bear it! Come on, Viv, relax," he groaned, his tongue wandering round her ear. "Bugger Leonard Mantlepiece. Let's stay here for a bit..."

"No! I'm not staying here for any 'bit'!" she insisted. "Now come on downstairs! Now!" She pointed towards the door. "You're like a big baby!"

"What about your shelf. Can't I fix it for you?"

The Cheese Murder

"Another time when we're not on duty! Now go on! Get down those stairs!"

He sulkily got up, hunched with disappointment and skulked off. She slapped him on the backside as he passed her. She smiled and followed him down.

They arrived at Cobblestone Street around two o'clock, repeatedly clattering on Len's door.

"Hold on! Hold on!" came a distant cry followed by the sound of thumping as Leonard descended the stairs. He opened the door, cigarette drooping out of his mouth, tucking his shirt in his jeans and zipping up his flies. His hair was wildly ruffled, his face hot and red.

"Oh, it's you," he mumbled. He reluctantly allowed them access.

"Come at a bad time?" Fluids grinned.

"You could say that," Len replied, flattening his mis-shapen fringe.

"Who is it?" Chris called from upstairs.

"Plod!"

"Oh." She appeared on the landing and came down to greet the officers, similarly dishevelled. "Hello, officers."

"Sorry for the intrusion but we have a few final questions," said Vivian.

"Bugger!" shouted Leonard, looking at his watch. "It's two o'clock, Chris!"

"Is it? Sorry, officers but we've got to dash round to Church Lane. We've got someone coming to view the house. They'll be arriving any time now. Sorry."

They scuttled around searching for their shoes.

"Can we wait here for you? Will you be long'?" asked Fluids.

"Oh... yes, okay...I suppose..." Len flapped, grabbing his keys. "See you back here in ten minutes or so then... " And the couple ran out the door.

"Frisky, aren't they?" commented Vivian.

The Cheese Murder

"Mmm," nodded Brian moving to grab her.

"No Brian!" She slapped his hand and turned away. "Now let's have a look round while we're here."

"What are we looking for?"

"I don't know, sir. There may be something, some clue somewhere."

They carefully rummaged, inspecting the cupboards.

"Does Christine smoke'?" asked the Inspector, finding a pile of gold packs.

"I don't think so."

"He's well stocked up, then. All duty frees," he observed.

"Duty frees?" she questioned, looking round.

"Yes. Look."

"Maybe someone brought them back for him. Crumblewick and Teeth might know. We'll ask one of them when we've finished."

They continued searching, respectfully replacing everything.

Leonard and Christine returned. "Sorry about that," said Leonard.

"That's okay," smiled Fledgling. "We're off now, anyway."

"Oh? Didn't you want to ask us some questions?" queried Christine, puzzled.

"No, it can wait," she said. She signalled to an equally baffled Fluids.

"Oh yes, just one thing, Chris," she asked as she reached for the door.

"Yes?"

"Do you smoke?"

"No. But Len does."

"Thanks. Bye."

The officers walked to their car. "What are you up to, Viv?" asked the Inspector. "Why the rush to leave?"

"My holiday, sir. My holiday date's been moved," she said cryptically.

The Cheese Murder

"You've lost me. I don't quite know what you're up to," he said, turning the ignition and shaking his head in bewilderment.

Evening came. Leonard and Christine walked arm-in-arm round to the Grinning Plank. Reg and Bob came in and joined them.

An hour passed, the foursome enjoying their Baggin's Old Blagger, Slapper's Weasel and Malibu, commenting on the pleasant atmosphere.

"It's no quieter though, is it?" observed Reg. "It's as noisy as ever - it's just the tone of the place. No hassle."

"Yeah," joked Bob. "No phone calls about cod and rice pudding or... or what was that other classic, Chris? Tripe Lasagne!"

They all laughed.

"I made some hideous meals, didn't I?" she smiled. "I really don't know why. It just seemed right at the time! I could never be bothered going into town to the supermarket. Do you know, I once made him a three course meal, a real candlelit affair."

They all nodded. "What was it?"

"The starter was a soup, Pea and Branston Pickle..." They laughed. "Then the main course was meant to be Chilli Con Carne but I was short of mince, so I made it with mashed up faggots..."

"Uggh!" they groaned, tongues exposed.

"And then pudding was Prune and Tapioca Crumble!"

"Yuck!" they spat in uproar.

"Did he eat it?" asked Reg, beaming across his globular face. "Nope. None. He went..."

"Down the pub!! they exclaimed in unison, their humour reaching fever pitch.

Constable Crumblewick came in. He approached Bert, the landlord, looked over and pointed. He came over to the table.

The Cheese Murder

"You're Bob Rack are you?" he asked, standing over him.
"Yes?"

"Could you come with me, please?"

"Eh?" Bob looked puzzled and red. The Constable clutched his arm and silently led him out of the pub. The laughter ceased. The table of three was dead silent.

"What's going on?" breathed Reg, his jaw dropping, his round face turning to oval.

"Surely he's not..?" exclaimed Chris.

They continued to drink, sitting mostly in shocked silence. The secrecy of Bob's exit, the uncertainty and suspense, had staggered them.

Another hour passed. Bert called time and the trio, worse-for-wear, got up to go.

A few sirens wailed outside, the noise increasing, getting closer and then stopped. A moment's silence. Four doors slammed shut. The pub door rattled open. Fluids and Fledgling strode in. Crumblewick and Bob followed.

Detective Inspector Fluids approached the three friends, the other officers standing behind him.

"Leonard Mantlepiece, I'm arresting you for the murder of Ralph Parmesan. Anything you say..."

"What are you on about?!" stormed Christine, standing between Len and Fluids, protecting him. *"You're mad!"*

Christine turned and grabbed Leonard. *"Its crap! Leaonard! Tell them they're wrong!"* she screamed, shaking him like a rag doll.

"We were round your house earlier today, weren't we, Leonard?" continued Fledgling. "We noticed you had 28 packs of duty free cigarettes. Your friends only bought you 20 packs. Explain that?"

"I don't know! Perhaps someone else bought him some as well as me and Bob!" Christine cried, continuing to push, pull and judder Leonard's limp, sullen body for reaction.

"And then we got Bob here to check the list of passengers who boarded the minibus for the France Trip on the Monday.

The Cheese Murder

You see, your lover went a day earlier to avoid suspicion. He wasn't ill at all!"

"Monday? There wasn't a bus on Monday!" she yelled. *"It was Tuesday!"*

"There *was* a bus on Monday. It went from Fumbleton, just three miles away."

"Yes, but his car? His car was at home..." she trembled, her eyes bloated and aching with sorrow, panic and disbelief.

"The bicycle. You borrowed Pierre's for a few days, didn't you, Mr Mantlepiece, knowing he only used it at weekends? You walked round there early on Monday morning and cycled to Fumbleton. That's why you left a message with your boss so very early. Because you had to get to Fumbleton to catch the 7:30 minibus."

"You knew about Parmesan's plans, didn't you, Mantlepiece? What he was going to buy in Calais, what his movements were going to be all day?" continued Fledgling. "Christine told you last Sunday night in here. You went to France on Monday getting the minibus from Fumbleton where no-one would know you. Then on Tuesday evening you cycled round to Church Lane. You knew bicycle tracks would put us off the scent. Then you poked the key through the back door, didn't you, and waited outside in the dark for Ralph to come home..."

Crumblewick joined in: "And you cunningly wore over-size boots! Then you let yourself in when Parmesan fell asleep. And you murdered him with some cheese!"

"You wanted Christine back so desperately, you just couldn't wait, could you?" fired Fluids. "You couldn't stand it! You couldn't put up with Parmesan's abuse any longer, could you? Your greed and desire became overpowering, didn't it, Mister Mantlepiece? You murdered him! A cold blooded murder by horrific suffocation. You killed a man with some cheese! A devilish plot! A cold blooded, devilish plot...!"

The words echoed and rebounded around Len's brain, blurring amongst a fog of wild, random emotions. The six pints

The Cheese Murder

of Slapper's and the discovery of his guilt mixed and muddled in his head. His mouth turned dry, his throat blocking a stream of words. Words of admission. Words of apology. Words to explain a mistake. A disastrous mistake. If only he'd known Chris was coming back. If only he'd waited one more day. An unnecessary murder. A murder out of overwhelming love. A murder that, in the end would lose him his lover for eternity, not regain her.

A most lovable man, destroyed. A future with nothing but years of incarceration and regret. A future of nothing without Christine. A future of hideous solitude. A Nothingness.

A weakness had enveloped him. His legs swayed, his arms drooped. His muscles caved in, his strength eroded. Reg grabbed him as he fell.

"Oh, my God!" Christine Ribcage shrieked, pulling viciously at her hair. *"Why the hell didn't I tell him?. Why didn't I let him know in time? Now I've got no-one!"* She screeched. She bawled. Awash with a torrent of tears.

Then Bob began to weep: "I'm sorry, Len, I'm sorry, I'm so sorry!" wracked with guilt over aiding the police.

Reg lay Leonard on the floor.

Leonard silently turned onto his side and curled himself up tight, his arms wrapped around his head. He wanted to hide himself away. His enthusiasm and zest for a perfect life had drained in that split second.

The three good friends knelt over his curled up, pathetic body, lamenting the loss of their greatest pal, a young man they'd always adored. Adored for his integrity. For his honesty. His warm heart. His humour. His gentility.

His Passion.

His Wretched Passion.

The Cheese Murder